THE TIME TRAVEL DIARIES

Previous series by
Caroline Lawrence

The Roman Mysteries
The Roman Mystery Scrolls
The Roman Quests
The P.K. Pinkerton Mysteries

THE TIME TRAVEL DIARIES

Caroline Lawrence

Piccadilly
PRESS

First published in Great Britain in 2019 by
PICCADILLY PRESS
80–81 Wimpole St, London W1G 9RE
www.piccadillypress.co.uk

A CIP catalogue record for this book is available from the British Library.

ISBN: 978-1-84812-800-2
Also available as an ebook

1

This book is typeset by Perfect Bound Ltd
Printed and bound in Great Britain by Clays Ltd, Elcograf S.p.A.

Piccadilly Press is an imprint of Bonnier Books UK
www.bonnierbooks.co.uk

To everyone at MOLA (Museum of London Archaeology), London Mithraeum Bloomberg SPACE and the Museum of London for their enthusiasm, expertise and support.

N

CRIPPLEGATE

FORT

NEWGATE

AMPHITHEATRE

RIVER FLEET

CHEAPSIDE
BATHS

LUDGATE

BATH HOUSE

RIVER THAMES

LONDINIUM
c. 260AD

CITY WALLS

BISHOPSGATE

CEMETERY

CITY WALLS

WALBROOK

BASILICA

ALDGATE

TEMPLE OF
MITHRAS

FORUM

SOUTHWARK

1
Blue Friday

When I went back in time to look for the blue-eyed girl with the ivory knife, I never thought I would actually find her. The only reason I took the job was for the money.

My adventure started on a cold day in January, the Friday before Blue Monday, officially the most depressing day in the year. A pile of dead Christmas trees tried to trip me up as I came out of my stairwell. I had been up late playing a computer game and overslept and missed breakfast. Then at break time Dinu Balan grabbed my packet of salt-and-vinegar crisps before I'd had even one. (No, I didn't fight him; he's about twice my size.)

So I was really looking forward to lunch.

But a few minutes before the bell rang, the school secretary came into the classroom and gave our teacher a slip of paper. Mrs Eckardt looked at the paper and then at me.

'Alexander,' she said, 'the headteacher wants to see you right away.'

'Uh-oh!' chanted some of the kids, and Dinu said, 'Are you in trouble, Wimpy?'

For the record, my name is not 'Wimpy'. Some of the kids call me that because I am a bit small for my age.

Everybody was staring at me like I'd committed a crime.

I glared back at them as I stood up.

I'm usually good-tempered, but I get cranky when I'm hungry. And I was ravenous.

I followed the secretary down the corridor and through the outer office. She tapped on the headteacher's door and opened it a crack.

'Alexander Papas to see you,' she said.

'Send him in,' came Miss Okonmah's voice. She was sitting at her desk. The window behind her let in a lot of cold winter light, which made her bushy grey hair look like the steel wool I use to scrub pans when I do the washing up.

'Please sit down, Alex,' she said.

I perched on the front of the chair, ready for a quick getaway if necessary. 'Am I in trouble, miss?'

'On the contrary; I might have an extraordinary opportunity for you. I just need to know a few things. Do you still do the lunchtime Latin club?'

'Yes, miss.'

'How is your Latin?'

'Pretty good. Miss Forte says I'm good at it because I know Greek so the language part of my brain is bigger.'

'You speak Greek?'

I nodded. 'I live with my gran. She's from Greece and we usually spend the summer with my aunt near Athens.'

'Of course.' She made a note on a piece of paper. 'Remind me how old you are?'

'I'm twelve, miss. Nearly thirteen.'

'You're a bit small for your age, aren't you?'

I scowled at her. 'So what?'

'Don't be defensive, Alex,' she said. 'That's a good thing in this case. And how are your teeth?'

'My teeth?' I frowned, wondering where this line of questioning was headed.

'Do you have any fillings?'

'No, miss.'

'You're sure?'

'Have a look,' I opened my mouth as wide as I could.

I did it sarcastically, but to my surprise she actually stood up, leaned forward and peered into my mouth. I could smell coffee on her breath.

'Excellent.' She sat down again and made another note. 'You like learning about the Romans, don't you?'

I shrugged. 'Sure. Also the Vikings and the Egyptians. But the Romans are my favourite.'

She put down her pen and looked at me. 'If given the

chance, Alex, would you like to go back to ancient Roman times?'

Ding! An imaginary light bulb lit up over my head. Hassan in the year above had got a part as an extra in a film a while ago. They paid him fifty pounds for just standing around with a bunch of other people and he got to miss a whole day of school. I guessed someone was looking for extras in a Roman movie. Or maybe even a kid actor with lines and everything.

'Yes, miss,' I said. 'It would be brilliant.'

'And your family could use some extra income?'

'Yes, miss. My gran lives on her pension.' My heart was thudding. If I could work as an extra for a whole week, I could earn two hundred and fifty pounds, maybe more. I could buy the latest smartphone. Plus the filmmakers might send me somewhere sunny and warm, on location. This could be my chance to break into movies and become rich and famous. This could be the beginning of my brilliant career!

My thoughts were tumbling over each other and Miss Okonmah had to snap her fingers to get my attention.

'Alexander,' she said, 'I asked if you can find your way around London.'

'Yes, miss,' I said. 'I help my gran with shopping and errands and stuff. I go all over on the bus and tube and train. On my own,' I added.

4

She looked at me for a moment, then took a small card and handed it to me.

'Can you go to this address tomorrow at noon?'

It was a business card, with black letters on cream. It said: *Solomon Daisy, Daisy Chain Enterprises, The Daisy Building, 7 Walbrook, London EC4N 4TA.*

The next day was Saturday. I usually cleaned our flat in the morning and then kicked a football around up at the common in the afternoon or went on my PlayStation if it was raining. But if this meant a chance to be in films I would happily move a few things around.

'Yes, miss. I can do that.'

'Good luck then,' she said. 'Make sure you're on time. Punctuality shows a potential employer that you are reliable. Now, you'd better get to lunch before all the fish fingers and chips have gone.'

'Thanks, miss.' I stood up and put the card in my back pocket.

'Oh, Alex?'

I turned with my hand already on the doorknob. 'Yes?'

'Don't tell a soul about this, not your friends or even your grandmother. It might jeopardise the deal.'

Here's a tip for you: if your headteacher sends you on a mission and warns you not to tell your parents or legal guardian about it, something is fishy.

2
Daisy Chain

The Daisy Building is located in London's financial district, between Cannon Street railway station and Bank tube. When I came up out of the underground, it was like I could see the past and the future all mashed up together. There was the Bank of England, looking like a temple dedicated to money. Crowded up behind it were glass-and-metal skyscrapers. I spotted the one that looks like a gherkin and one like a walkie-talkie and one that looks like a shard of glass.

I was disappointed that the Daisy Building didn't look like a giant daisy, but I guess that would be hard to pull off. It was just a curvy building of glass and steel about ten storeys tall.

Inside, three blond receptionists (all male) sat behind a desk made of pale yellow wood. They all wore the same dark jackets, white shirts and thin yellow neckties. For a moment

I wondered if they were triplets. Or maybe even clones.

When I handed the business card to Clone One he lifted an eyebrow and looked me up and down. 'And you are . . . ?'

'Alexander Papas,' I said. 'I was told to be here at noon. I'm from Wandsworth Academy.'

He touched a button and spoke into his headpiece. 'A schoolboy named Alexander Papas to see you, sir.' He nodded and pointed behind me. 'Take that lift to the top floor,' he said to me. 'Mr Daisy is expecting you.'

It was a state-of-the art lift with brushed steel and blond wood but no buttons that I could see. The doors had closed and I was wondering what to do when it started moving up on its own. After a few seconds the doors opened straight into a room with a huge curved window that looked out over the roofs of buildings, including one with a dome and a cross on top that I was pretty sure was St Paul's Cathedral. There was a plush white carpet and some shiny blocks of black marble with ancient-looking objects on them. One was a Greek vase with red warriors fighting on a black background. There was a bronze Egyptian-style cat with a gold earring in one ear. But what really caught my eye was a life-sized gilded breastplate like Roman soldiers used to wear. If it wasn't real then it was an excellent replica. Either way, this film was going to be a quality production.

'Alexander,' said a voice, and I turned to see a man sitting behind a desk. He had black-rimmed glasses and bushy black hair sprinkled with grey. I recognised Solomon Daisy from having googled him the night before. I knew that he was a super-wealthy businessman whose great-grandfather Reuben Denisovich had fled persecution in Russia around the year 1900. Somewhere between Moscow and London, Denisovich got shortened to 'Daisy'.

His business empire had been built on various modern inventions like computer chips and stuff. But he had made most of his money out of an affordable Virtual Reality visor.

'I'm Solomon Daisy,' said Solomon Daisy. 'Nice to meet you, Alexander.' He pushed himself up out of a big leather chair and extended his hand across the desk.

His desk was far enough away that I had time to look him up and down as I trotted over. His belly stretched against a grey T-shirt size XXXL. I was surprised he wasn't wearing a business suit, but my research had told me he was an eccentric bazillionaire, and I supposed eccentric bazillionaires could wear whatever they liked.

'Call me Alex,' I said. His hand was warm and moist but I did not flinch and gave it a firm squeeze.

'Good grip,' he said, sitting down with a grunt. 'I like that. Take a seat, please.'

I sat down. The leather chair was yellow, the colour of butter and just as soft.

'What do you want in life, Alex?' said Solomon Daisy.

I shrugged. 'Same thing every other kid in my class wants. To be rich and famous.'

Solomon Daisy shook his big head. 'Nobody strives for excellence any more,' he said sadly. And then, 'How would you like to earn a million pounds?'

I nearly slipped off the butter-soft leather chair.

'For a movie?' My voice cracked a little.

'What?' It was his turn to be confused.

'You want me to be in a movie about ancient Rome, right? Or maybe a VR game?'

'What gave you that idea?'

'My headteacher said something about time travel back to ancient Rome.'

'And that's exactly what I want you to do. Time travel. But not back to ancient Rome. To Roman London. And I'll pay you a million pounds.'

'For a virtual-reality game?'

'Not virtual reality. Real reality. I want you to literally go back in time.'

I stared at him for a moment and then swallowed. His glasses reflected the buildings of the City of London and made it hard for me to see his eyes. But he seemed serious.

'It's dangerous,' he explained. 'That's why the payment is so much. But if you make the journey to the past, you get the money whether you return or not.'

'Whether I return or not?' I echoed stupidly.

9

I looked around for the hidden camera, or maybe a comedian to jump out from behind the Roman breastplate and yell, *'Bazinga!'*

Solomon Daisy gave a wheezy laugh. 'You don't believe me,' he said, 'but it's true. Time travel is not a thing of the future. It's here now. I invented it last year. Or rather some of my tech people did.'

I realised the guy must be crazy and that I had to get out fast. But the elevator was a good ten metres from my chair and it had no buttons inside. My only chance was to play along until I could escape. Maybe I could make a joke of it all.

He was watching me with his bushy black eyebrows raised.

I said, 'How can you travel back in time?'

'I could tell you –' he began.

'– but then you'd have to kill me?' I was only half kidding.

He gave a single snort of laughter. 'Nah. I could tell you, but it would take an hour or two, and you wouldn't understand anyway.'

I stood up. 'Excuse me, Mr Daisy, but I have to go back to planet Earth.'

He stood up too, and I would have been worried except for the fact that his face was genuinely beaming. 'Alex,' he said, 'have you heard of the Roman god Mithras?'

'Sure,' I said. 'We were talking about that in Latin club last week. He was a strange Roman god whose worshippers did mysterious things. They discovered his temple somewhere around here when they were cleaning up rubble after the Blitz. My teacher said they recently re-opened the Temple of Mithras on its original site.'

Solomon Daisy clapped his meaty hands in delight. 'Exactly!' he cried. 'And I'm going to show you why it's the perfect place for a time portal.'

3

London Mithraeum

'Come,' said the cheerful madman named Solomon Daisy. 'Come have a look at the Temple of Mithras. It's right across the way.' He led the way to the lift and I saw he was wearing plus-sized Levi's jeans and black trainers.

I followed at a safe distance.

As we passed the Greek vase I couldn't resist asking, 'Is it real?'

'Yes. It's worth half a million pounds.'

'Did you go back in time to ancient Greece to get it?'

'No.' He pushed a button on a plinth to call the lift. 'When you travel back in time you can't take anything with you. And you can't bring anything back. I bought the vase at Christies,' he added. 'In an auction.'

The doors of the lift opened with a hiss and he gestured for me to go first. 'Also,' he said, following me in, 'adults can't travel in time, only pre-pubescent children.'

I wasn't sure what 'pre-pubescent' meant, but it sounded creepy. The lift doors closed and I held my breath. If he was going to try anything, now would be the perfect moment. I got ready to kick him between the legs. But the lift doors were already opening again to reveal the three blond clones and people walking around.

I heaved a sigh of relief.

'This way,' he said, heading for the main doors. It was drizzling outside but we only had to cross a pedestrian walkway before we entered another set of glass doors. It looked like a modern art gallery, not a temple. Two women with cheerful smiles stood by a podium. Each held the latest version of a clipboard, a white touch tablet.

'Welcome to London Mithraeum,' said the taller one. 'Have you pre-booked?'

'Mr Daisy doesn't need to book!' whispered the shorter one. 'He owns the building across the street and comes here most days.'

'Sorry, sir!' The first woman's cheeks went bright pink. 'The next immersive experience is in five minutes, if you and your son want to go down right away. Or take this touch tablet which has information about the six hundred Roman artefacts on the wall.'

Solomon Daisy waved a chubby hand. 'We'll look at the artefacts later,' he said, and led the way past a wall of Roman artefacts behind glass.

He stopped at the top of some stairs, and so did I.

The narrow stairwell was lined on both sides with shiny black marble, which made it look spooky, like going down into a tomb. But the gallery attendants were there so I guessed I was safe.

Unless I slipped and took a tumble.

Or was pushed.

4
Beam Me Back

As I stood at the top of the black marble stairs going down, I felt a prickle at the back of my neck. I stepped aside.

'After you,' I said to the mad bazillionaire.

As I followed Solomon Daisy down, I saw that different ground levels had been etched into the black marble walls flanking the stairs. '1941 WORLD WAR II BOMBING DESTROYS MOST OF THE BUILDINGS ON THIS SITE' read one inscription by a horizontal line. A little further down the wall told me, '1666 THE GREAT FIRE OF LONDON'. And near the bottom I saw: '1066 WILLIAM THE CONQUEROR IS CROWNED IN LONDON'.

'At almost every ancient site in the world,' said Solomon Daisy over his shoulder, 'when you go down, you go back in time.'

I felt a surge of relief. 'Oh!' I said. 'So *this* is the time machine. Going down into the basement.'

'No,' he said as we came into a black room. 'This isn't the time machine. We're just going down to the level of third-century London. And we're not quite there yet. This is just the mezzanine.'

I had no idea what a mezzanine was, but I saw that the room held three displays, one of which I recognised as a white resin cast of the head of Mithras, the one they found after the Blitz. I wanted to have a closer look, but a male guide in black was beckoning us towards more stairs leading down from the far side of the room.

'Please go down now if you want the immersive experience,' he said.

Once again I let Solomon Daisy go first. At the lowest level some black double doors opened into a dimly lit underground space. Here were the foundations of an ancient temple surrounded by a walkway and a low glass barrier. There were about twelve other people already in there, tourists by the look of it.

The walls of the space containing the ruins were black and so was the ceiling. Spotlights lit the temple foundations from above. Outside, the January day was damp and chilly, but down here it was dry and warm.

'This is the best place to stand,' said Solomon Daisy. He led me out onto a central walkway like the one models strut down during a fashion show. One of the spotlights lit the top of his bushy black hair and cast his face into shadow.

Frankly the ruins looked a bit dull. Just a big stone rectangle, a dirt floor and a curved bit at the far end.

Crazy Daisy pointed over the glass barrier to the far end of the temple foundations, where a big semicircular pane of glass showed a man in a floppy hat and fluttering cloak stabbing a bull. The way the lights shone made the figure glow against the black wall beyond.

'That etching of Mithras,' said Solomon Daisy, 'is meant to suggest the cult statue. Experts think the statue was plaster and only the head was marble.'

'The bull's not very big, is it?' I said. 'More like a big dog than a bull . . . Also, he's not even looking at it.'

Daisy nodded. 'It's a puzzle,' he agreed. 'There are over two hundred representations of Mithras killing the bull, all more or less like that. But we know almost nothing about the cult of Mithras or what his followers did in a temple like this. It's as if we had images of a man on a cross but no New Testament to tell us what Christianity was all about.'

I peered over the glass partition down into the rectangular foundations below us.

'Is this the whole temple?' I asked. 'Our school cafeteria is bigger.'

'This is it,' said Solomon Daisy. 'It's the same design as many churches, with a central nave and two side aisles. We think that after every service they reclined on the side sections and enjoyed a banquet.'

I nodded slowly. 'It does look a bit like my gran's church. With the centre bit for pews.'

'Only they didn't have pews in ancient times,' said Solomon Daisy. 'That space was left empty unless there happened to be a ceremony. Which makes it the perfect place for a portal.'

'Why does it have to be empty?' I asked.

'Have you ever seen the TV series *Star Trek*?'

'No, but I've seen the movies.'

'Then you know what a transporter is.'

'Beam me up?' I said.

'Exactly. What would happen if they beamed Captain Kirk into a wall?'

'He would die?'

'Horribly. To travel back in time you have to find a space that you're sure will be empty.'

I frowned. 'You could just go to a field or a beach, couldn't you?'

'You're forgetting the ground level,' he said. 'It generally rises over time. That black marble staircase we came in down illustrates it perfectly. Imagine if we placed the portal at today's street level. As you stepped through you would fall seven metres, probably breaking both legs. On the other hand, if we placed it too low, you'd step into solid earth and die. It's not just longitude and latitude we have to calculate, but altitude. There aren't many places where we know the exact three-dimensional coordinates for a specific time period. If

18

you want to go to third-century Roman London, then this Mithraeum is the perfect place to put a portable portal.'

This was beginning to make sense in a strange way.

I realised I was being sucked in.

Then everything went black.

5
Nama Mithras

I didn't panic when we were plunged into darkness seven metres below street level.

I figured it was part of the London Mithraeum 'immersive experience'.

But just to be safe I took a step back from Crazy Daisy.

For a moment everyone was quiet. Then, somewhere in the darkness, I heard a door squeak open followed by men's voices and footsteps crunching on gravel. Were actors coming? No. It was recorded sound effects being played over a loudspeaker.

An animal horn blared, and behind us a slab of light appeared where the main entrance of the temple would have been. While we had been in darkness they had filled the room with mist, which was now illuminated wherever lights shone down.

Clever.

More lights came on, their beams forming the walls of the

Mithraeum. Hanging pieces of wood made seven shadowed gaps on each side, showing where the columns would have been. I heard a drum and then the voices of men chanting in Latin.

I caught the word *leonibus*. Something about lions. Then *patri* – 'to the father'. And the word *nama* over and over. '*Nama Mithras!*' came the voices of the unseen worshippers. '*Nama Mithras!*'

The drumming got faster and faster until it stopped. A flute trilled and the image of Mithras stabbing the bull lit up.

I heard men chatting and the clink of metal cups or forks on plates. That must be the banquet part.

Finally came a loud creak of hinges and the sound of a door closing and . . . the wind. (Mrs Eckardt says the wind always stands for desolation and abandonment.)

It was cheesy, but effective. I have to admit a little shiver ran down my spine as the lights came up.

Solomon Daisy looked around, and seemed surprised to see me standing some distance from him. He raised his eyebrows as if to ask if I was impressed.

I gave him a thumbs-up, which they might or might not have done in Roman times. For the first time it really hit me: what if I *could* go back to Roman London?

I'd be able to see what a ceremony to Mithras was really like. I could watch gladiators battle each other and maybe attend a chariot race. I could eat stuffed dormice and try the famous fish-gut sauce that Romans were mad about.

That last thought made my stomach growl. Thinking about food does that to me. Even thinking about disgusting food.

'Have you had lunch?' asked Solomon Daisy. 'I can tell you more about the project while we eat. There's a restaurant in Bloomberg Arcade that serves the best pizza in London. And for dessert we can swing by a hamburger place that does something called an Oreo milkshake.'

'You had me at lunch,' I said.

Solomon Daisy gave a snort of laughter. 'Good. I'll tell you about the person I want you to find, the blue-eyed girl with the ivory leopard knife.'

6

Floppy Pizza

We got a table for two at the restaurant, so close to the pizza oven that I could feel the heat on the right side of my face. Daisy somehow managed to squeeze his bulk between the table and his chair. The pizzas came in only one size, so we ordered half margherita for me, half mushroom and ricotta for him.

'I don't know if I'd survive long in Roman London,' I said as a pretty waitress delivered a massive pizza and two paper plates to our table. 'The Romans had no tomato for pizzas. Or chocolate. Or chilli peppers. Or potatoes for salt-and-vinegar crisps,' I added.

'It doesn't really matter what food they did or didn't have.' Daisy used the pizza wheel to cut eight big slices. 'You're not allowed to eat when you go back in time.'

'Not allowed to eat?' I paused with the first slice of pizza halfway to my mouth.

'Yup. Any food in your stomach will be violently expelled as you go through the portal.'

'Violently expelled as in . . . ?'

'Yup. Violently expelled through your "personal portals".' He grinned and rolled up a slice of pizza.

'Ugh!' I said. 'But how will I live if I can't eat?'

'People can survive for a surprisingly long time without food,' said Solomon Daisy. That was when he told me the three rules of time travel, counting them off on his already greasy fingers: *'One: naked you go and naked you must return. Two: drink, don't eat. Three: as little interaction as possible.'*

My jaw was hanging open.

'Of course, a skinny kid like you probably wouldn't last a month,' he went on. 'But don't worry – you'll only be there for three or four days. Five max. And of course you have to fast for two days before you make the jump. But I'm sure you can go without food for a week.'

'No food *for a week*?'

'Oh, and I suppose I should warn you about the shortened life expectancy.'

'Shortened what?'

Solomon Daisy extricated another section of pizza. 'In the normal course of events, the life expectancy for a boy like you is around ninety-five.'

'I'll live to be nearly a hundred?'

'Yup. Barring the zombie apocalypse and assuming you

don't walk in front of a bus, you can expect to live for another eighty-three years.' He dabbed his mouth with a paper napkin. 'However, my tech guys have calculated that for each hour you spend in the past, it takes a month off your life expectancy.'

I did the figures in my head. 'So that means if I spend a day in the past it will cut two years off my life?'

'Yup. Twenty-four months is the price for spending twenty-four hours in the past. That means you'll probably only live to be ninety-three. It's much worse for adults,' he said. 'Every hour *we* spend back in time cuts a *year* off our lifespan. It's something to do with cell regeneration.'

'So that's why you're not going yourself.'

'Exactly. May I try some of your pizza?'

'Sure,' I said, easing a slice onto his paper plate. 'I suppose I can face living to be ninety-two rather than ninety-five.' I chewed thoughtfully. 'Why did Miss Okonmah ask me if I had fillings?'

'My tech guys reckon that if you have anything non-organic in your head, like an ear stud or a filling, it would probably explode.'

7
Exploding Teeth

'So if I went through the portal with fillings . . .' I began, and then trailed off.

'Your head would probably explode!' He took a bite of the rolled-up pizza and tomato sauce squirted onto his cheek. 'A bit like that!' he grinned, and then wiped his face with the paper napkin.

'And that's also why I have to go through naked?'

'Yup,' he said.

'But aren't clothes made out of organic material? Like cotton and wool?'

'My tech guys think any clothes you're wearing will go up in flames . . .' He took a big bite. 'They're not sure why. Do you want to be our guinea pig?'

'I guess not. But *naked* . . .'

'Don't worry. Romans had a more relaxed attitude to nudity. All you have to do is find some clothes as soon as you arrive. There should be some priestly robes in an anteroom of the Mithraeum.'

For some reason all this talk of exploding heads and shortened life expectancy actually made me feel better. It seemed as if his tech guys really knew what they were doing. I helped myself to a slice of his mushroom-and-ricotta pizza and thought about it all as I ate.

'And you want me to find a blue-eyed girl?'

'That's right. She was buried in Southwark.'

'Where's Sutherk?' I asked.

'It's spelled South-Wark but pronounced Sutherk,' said Solomon Daisy. 'It was the industrial part of Londinium, which as I'm sure you know is what the Romans called London, and was located just across the river. It was very marshy, with workshops, kilns and other noisy or smelly activities. There were a few small islands in that part of south London. Some of them were used as cemeteries.'

'Because Romans buried their dead outside the town walls.'

'Yes. Have you been to Shakespeare's Globe Theatre?'

I nodded. 'It's near the Tate Modern.'

'They were clearing the ground for some new apartments about half a mile south of there and they found several graves. The richest one belonged to a fourteen-year-old girl.'

'So did she do something terrible? Like kill somebody or invent a virus? And I have to go back to stop her?'

'No,' he said. 'She was just an ordinary girl as far as we can tell. We know from the DNA in her bones that she had blue eyes and looked like a northern European. But the isotopes in her teeth suggest that she grew up in north Africa. She was only nine when she came to Londinium. She died five years later, aged fourteen.'

'If we can tell so much about her from her bones and DNA and teeth and stuff,' I said, 'and if she didn't do anything terrible, then why do you need me to go back and find her?'

'Simple,' he said, tucking into his fifth piece of pizza. 'I'm obsessed with her. Can't stop thinking about her. And once I had this really vivid dream. I have to know what brought her three thousand miles from Africa to Britain. And why she died.'

'And you'll pay me a million pounds just to go back and try to find her?'

'Did I mention a four-million bonus if you actually locate her?'

I nearly choked on my pizza. '*Five* million pounds?'

He beamed. 'Yes! If you find the blue-eyed girl from Africa, then you get five mil.'

'Is everything all right?' asked our waitress. I noticed she had bright blue eyes and took that as a good omen.

'Yes,' I said happily. 'Everything is very all right.'

8
Butterfly Thunder

'So,' I repeated about ten minutes later, 'you'll pay me a million pounds to go back to Roman London, and if I find the blue-eyed girl buried in Southwark, you'll give me another four million pounds as a bonus?'

'Yup,' said Solomon Daisy.

We had just bought two Oreo milkshakes from Bloomberg Arcade and we were sitting beside a bronze water sculpture that showed what the ancient Walbrook stream might have looked like in Roman times.

'Blue eyes is not a lot to go on,' I said. 'Are there any other clues I can use to find her? Do we at least know her name? Like from her tombstone?'

'No tombstone,' he said, 'but we have some fascinating grave goods.'

'What are "grave goods"?'

'Things buried with a body. Most ancient people believed

in life after death. They sometimes left objects with the body to help them make the journey to the next world.'

'Like a coin in the mouth to pay the ferryman.' I took a suck of my shake.

'Exactly,' said Solomon Daisy. 'Grave goods often help us figure out who the person was, where they came from and when they died. The blue-eyed girl was buried with two glass perfume jars, a small wooden box, a small key on a chain and the ivory knife.'

'Ah,' I said. 'The famous knife.'

Crazy Daisy put down his milkshake, pulled out a smartphone and tapped up a photo. 'These are the things that were found with her.'

I put down my cup too and took the phone. The first photo on the screen showed two little perfume jars. Next was a key and section of chain.

'Is the key bronze?' I asked, making an educated guess.

'Yes, although we call it copper-alloy these days,' he said. 'The wooden box was placed at her feet. It had bone decoration and copper-alloy fittings, but strangely no sign of a lock.'

'So the key wasn't for that?'

'Apparently not. If you find her, ask about the key.'

I tapped the phone.

The next object looked like a folding penknife.

'It looks like a folding penknife,' I said.

'That's exactly what it is,' he said. 'The handle is ivory, carved in the shape of a leopard. Ivory was very exotic and expensive back then, because it is made of elephant's tusk. The blade is iron, very corroded now. Of course, the Romans had no pockets. We think it might have hung from her belt along with the key.'

I finished my milkshake and put the cup down. 'There's something else I'm wondering about,' I said. 'Time crash. In *Star Trek* and *Back to the Future* they're always worrying about disrupting the space–time continuum.'

'Yes,' he said. *'A Sound of Thunder.'*

I gazed up at the sky. The clouds had cleared and it was a pale blue. 'I don't hear anything.'

'No. It's the name of a science-fiction short story by Ray Bradbury from the 1950s. In the story, some time travellers go back to the time of dinosaurs. They are warned not to touch anything or interact with the world, as even the tiniest change in the past could cause bigger and bigger changes that over centuries could affect the course of the future.'

'And?'

'One of them steps on a butterfly and kills it. When they get back to their own time they have a different president.'

'So I'm not allowed to kill any butterflies?'

'Kill as many bugs as you like,' said Daisy, 'but keep human interaction to a minimum. Rule number three, remember?

However, we have made three trips back to Roman London, and Donald Trump is still president. My tech guys reckon that the effect of any trip back has already been accounted for in the present.'

'That does my head in,' I said. And then, 'Three trips to the past? What happened to the travellers?'

'Three trips but just one traveller. He's alive and well,' said Daisy. 'And fabulously rich.' He chuckled. 'He actually is a Traveller.'

'What do you mean?'

'It's what they used to call Irish gypsies. A few of them still live a life close to that of the ancient Romans. They know how to milk a goat and kindle a fire. That kind of stuff.'

'Do you think I could meet him?' I asked.

'Most certainly. If you pass the audition.'

'Audition?'

He gave me a piece of paper with an address. 'I want you to go to this wine bar on Tuesday evening. Six o'clock. Don't be late.'

'I may look eighteen,' I said, 'but I'm only twelve.'

Solomon Daisy gave a snort of laughter. 'Once a month,' he said, 'a few grown-up Latin geeks gather there over dinner. They meet in a private room downstairs, so you shouldn't have any trouble getting in. But you have to speak only in Latin – not one word of English.'

He must have seen the look of panic on my face because

he said, 'They serve good burgers there.'

'*Optime*,' I said, which means 'excellent'. I was trying to think of the Latin word for hamburger.

'If you decide to audition for the gig, the phone is yours to keep, whether you pass or not. And if they give you their seal of approval, then you're good to go.'

'So I've got the job?' I said.

'Yes,' he said. 'If the geeks give you the thumbs up, I'll take you to meet our Traveller, and then send you back seventeen hundred years.'

'When?' I said. 'When will I go through the portal?' My mouth was suddenly as dry as fresh sawdust in a hamster cage.

'Friday morning,' he said. 'Or as soon as Tuesday's meal passes through your system.'

'You mean next Tuesday's meal with the Latin geeks might be the last food I eat before I travel back in time?'

'Yup,' said Solomon Daisy. 'That will be your last supper.'

9
Trailblazer

My decision to order a hamburger at the Latin Circle audition had proved to be a wise one. Every time one of the geeks asked me a difficult question, I would take a bite and chew slowly while I worked out what to say. If I didn't understand the question I replied, '*Minime*,' which means 'Not at all', and discourages further questioning.

When I showed up at the Daisy Building on Wednesday morning, I found I had passed my audition with flying colours.

'They especially liked your phrase for hamburger,' said Solomon Daisy. I noticed there were two butter-soft leather chairs in front of his desk instead of just one.

'*Pastillum fartum!*' A smiling boy in jeans and a black hoodie limped out from behind one of the plinths where he had been lurking.

'Yup.' I grinned. 'According to Google, *pastillum fartum* is Latin for hamburger.'

'Alex, meet Martin, your predecessor,' said Solomon Daisy.

Martin was maybe a year older than I was. He had a long face, curly brown hair and eyes as black as his hoodie. He also had the beginnings of a moustache, which was probably why he was no longer a time traveller. He seemed a bit nervous, but his smile looked genuine and his handshake was firm.

Solomon Daisy said, 'Martin has been through the portal three times. He thinks he might have a clue about how to find the girl with the ivory knife.'

The boy sat in one of the butter-soft chairs. I sat in the other, facing him.

Martin said, 'On my second trip to Roman London, I found a man named Caecilius who sells objects made of ivory.'

'Caecilius like in the *Cambridge Latin Course*?'

Martin looked startled and then shrugged. 'I don't know what that is. Anyway, his shop is on the south side of the river between a big bath house and a fullers'. Do you know what a fullers' is?'

I shook my head.

Martin pulled an energy bar from his pocket and unwrapped it. 'The word in Latin is *fullonica*. It's where they clean clothes. They're pretty smelly because they use urine as part of the soaking process.'

'Urine?' I said. 'As in pee?'

'Yes,' said Martin. 'And they sometimes burn sulphur, which smells like rotten eggs. That means you don't even have to ask directions; just follow your nose.'

'So there's a man named Caecilius who sells knives near the pee laundry?'

'Yes. He sells folding knives made of bone and iron. Some of the handles are shaped like different animals but they all had the same kind of blade. I asked him the stock question . . .'

I recited one of the phrases I had memorised along with him: '*Puellam oculis caeruleis quaero et cultro eburneo.*' I seek a girl with blue eyes and an ivory knife.

Martin nodded. 'Caecilius the knife-seller didn't know her so I decided to ask if he had ever sold a knife with a handle shaped like a leopard. But I couldn't remember the word for leopard.'

'*Panthera maculata,*' I said. 'Or *leopardus.*'

Solomon Daisy's bushy eyebrows went up. 'Have you already learned all the words on the list I gave you?'

I nodded. 'I've also been listening to the Latin podcasts you recommended and I memorised your map of third-century Roman London. Anyway,' I said to Martin, '*panthera* and *leopardus* are both no-brainers.'

He gave a lopsided grin. 'I know,' he said. 'But I was pretty hungry. I'd been there for three days with no food and my brain was slow.' He took a big bite of his energy bar. My mouth watered and my tummy growled.

'Want one?' He reached into his pocket and pulled out another one.

I shook my head.

'He's on the prep fast,' said Solomon Daisy, and to me, 'By the way, Alex, don't rely on nodding and shaking your head when you go back. Gestures have different meanings in different cultures.'

'I know,' I said. 'In Greece they tip their head back for no and it looks like they're nodding.'

'That's right,' said Solomon Daisy. 'Shortly after the Second World War an English tourist was swimming in the waters between Corfu and Albania. He lost his bearings. Armed Albanian soldiers were gesturing for him to go away and he thought they were beckoning him on, so he swam towards them.'

'What happened?' I asked.

'They shot him dead.'

I swallowed hard.

'That's why I want you to lurk in the background. Just find the girl and observe.'

'*Rule three,*' I said, '*as little interaction as possible.*'

'But you will have to ask Caecilius if he ever sold a knife with an ivory-leopard handle,' said Martin. 'That will be your best lead.'

I said, 'You found Caecilius on your second trip?'

Martin nodded.

I frowned. 'Mr Daisy said you've made three trips back. If you had such a good clue, why didn't you ask him on your third trip?'

'I wasn't quite straight with you,' said Solomon Daisy. 'Martin did go back a third time. But we had to cut his visit short.'

'Why?' I asked. 'Did something go wrong?'

The two of them looked at each other. 'You could say that,' said Martin.

'It was a few months later,' said Solomon Daisy, 'and in that time they'd raised the floor level of the Mithraeum by putting in a new wooden floor. When Martin arrived there the third time, the sole of his right foot fused with the oak planks and they had to amputate.'

10
Cold Feet

'They had to amputate your foot?' I asked Martin. 'As in cut it off?'

'Yes.'

'Ouch!' I winced.

'It's not too bad,' said Martin, and pulled up the cuff of his jeans. 'They've given me a cyber-foot so at least I don't need to use crutches or a wheelchair any more.'

I tried not to seem horrified by the prosthetic ankle emerging from his shoe. 'You lost your whole foot?' I said.

Martin nodded. 'I managed to crawl back through. By the way,' he said, 'you have to go through the same side of the portal, like a revolving door. So I had to crawl around to the front and heave myself inside.'

Solomon Daisy said, 'We leave the portal on for five minutes in case you need to come back for any reason.'

'OK.' I was feeling queasy.

'I left a lot of blood in the Mithraeum,' said Martin, 'but once I got back to our time, they stopped the bleeding and rushed me to the hospital.'

'That's terrible!' I murmured.

Martin gave a brave shrug and took a sip of coffee. 'It's OK. Thanks to Mr Daisy I've got millions in the bank. I'll never have to work again. Also, every time scientists make an improvement, I can get a newer foot. It's in my contract.'

My stomach had been grumbling for breakfast. Now it shut up.

I looked accusingly at Solomon Daisy.

He held up both hands, palms outward. 'I'm ninety-nine per cent sure it won't happen to you. But if anything does go wrong, I will cover all medical treatment needed for as long as you live. In addition to a five-million-pound compensation payment. Right, Martin?'

'Right.' Martin grinned. 'I've bought a fleet of vintage Jetstream trailers for me and my family. The rest of the money is in the bank. I can live off the interest forever. Look!' He pulled back the sleeve of his black hoodie and I saw a chunky watch on his wrist.

'Rolex Skydweller,' he explained. 'Cost twenty thousand pounds.'

Solomon Daisy leaned forward and said, 'You don't need to be hurt to get rich, Alex. Remember the four-mil bonus if you find the girl.'

I nodded. I had been thinking of little else over the past few days.

'Tell me more about Roman London,' I said to Martin. 'What do I need to know?'

'Londinium is amazing.' Martin scratched his curly head. 'Everybody drives chariots and they all wear togas. You'll see soldiers marching and gladiators fighting. Oh, and here's how they shake hands.' He stretched out his right arm. When I went to shake it he said, 'No. Grab my forearm and I'll grab yours.'

'Oh yeah,' I said, grasping his arm just below the elbow. 'I think I've seen this in the movies.'

'That's right!' said Martin. 'It makes more sense than shaking hands,' he said, 'because you don't pass germs and viruses to people.'

I frowned. 'I thought ancient Romans didn't know about germs . . .'

Martin's smile vanished and he shrugged. 'Well, that's how they do it.'

'Do you have any practical advice for me?' I asked him. 'Like where to get clothes?'

'You'll find stuff in a room just inside the entrance of the temple,' said Martin. 'It's where the priests change. If you come through the portal during one of their ceremonies, stay hidden until it's over and they've gone. Don't make a peep. Even if you hear men cawing and roaring.'

I gave him a sharp look. 'Cawing and roaring?'

Martin nodded. 'Mithraism is a mystery cult and there are different levels, with a different avatar for each level, like the Raven, the Soldier –'

I interrupted. '– the Bridegroom, the Lion, the Persian, the Sun-Runner and the Father.' I had been reading up on what little was known about the cult.

Solomon Daisy clapped and said, 'Bravo, Alex! I knew we chose the right boy for the job.'

'Yes,' said Martin. 'And I heard them doing a strange thing where they click their tongues and whistle. Also, they shake rattles.'

'Rattles? Like baby rattles?'

Solomon Daisy answered for him. 'We think Martin heard a type of Egyptian rattle called a *sistrum*. Plural form: *sistra*. They look like bronze egg whisks with tiny cymbals or rods. They jingle when you shake them.'

I frowned. 'Why do they shake them?'

'We think some of the noises were to keep away evil spirits,' said Solomon Daisy.

'After they make strange signs and noises,' continued Martin, 'they perform a weird kind of ceremony. I was hiding behind the statue but I peeked. Some guys were wearing animal masks. I saw one that looked like a raven. And one man was naked and blindfolded.'

'What?' My jaw dropped.

'We think it was part of their initiation rite,' said Solomon Daisy.

'Then what happened?' I asked.

Martin shrugged. 'The guy with the raven mask turned his head, so I ducked back down. I was afraid if they saw me they might kill me.'

'Kill you?' My voice came out squeakier than I would have liked. 'Like a human sacrifice?'

'No. Because they might think I was a spy.'

I swallowed hard.

I had already started a list of Ways to Die in Londinium. Now I would have to add Death by Angry Priest of Mithras.

'Don't worry,' said Martin. 'I think I know one of their secret passwords: *Deus Sol Invictus Mithras*, which means "God is the Sun, is Unconquered, is Mithras".'

I nodded. 'Invictus like invincible. I can remember that.'

'I also heard some of them shout "*Stella sum!*"'

'What? "I am a star"?'

At this Solomon Daisy leaned forward. 'The whole point of the ceremony is to ensure that the immortal part of you, your soul, will go up to the stars after your earthly body dies. Have you ever heard of Plato's Cave?'

'No, but wasn't Plato the ancient Greek who wrote dialogues about philosophy?' I said.

'*Ita vero.* He's the man who made Socrates famous. Another person I'm obsessed with.'

'Did Plato live in a cave?'

'No. A character in one of his dialogues says our lives are like those of prisoners in a cave, watching torch-lit shadows on a wall and trying to make sense of the cosmos that way.'

'Cosmos? As in universe?'

'Yes. It's strange, but one of their models for the cosmos was a cave. That may be why the temples to Mithras had no windows. In fact they called them Caves of Mithras rather than "temples". One scholar believes the Mithraeum was like a driving simulator or a satnav. Lights and torches would show the worshippers the route their immortal souls needed to take after they died. Our young traveller here has thrown a lot of light on a very mysterious cult. Pun intended.'

Solomon Daisy beamed at Martin and then turned the spotlight of his smile on me. 'So! Are you still up for some time travel?'

I took a deep breath. 'I think so.'

'Good.' Solomon Daisy bent down and lifted up a battered briefcase. He put it on his lap, popped it open and produced a sheet of paper. 'Here's your contract. Read it carefully. As soon as you're ready, just sign on the dotted line.'

He handed me the sheet of paper and a fancy fountain pen, uncapped and ready to use.

I took the pen and put the contract on the table so that I could give it a quick scan. I ignored all the tiny type and just looked at the main points relevant to me:

Going through the portal – £1 million pounds.

Finding the Blue-eyed Girl with the Ivory Leopard Knife – £4 million bonus.

Loss of a limb – £5 million damages plus lifetime private care.

Death or Non-Return – £10 million pounds to Mrs Katerina Papas.

Seeing the word 'DEATH' alongside Gran's name made my innards twist like spaghetti on a fork. She would be devastated if I died.

I would be devastated if I died.

I put the top back on the pen without signing.

'Can I have a day to think about it?'

Solomon Daisy's smile faded from two hundred watts to about forty. Then he took a deep breath and screwed his smile back up to a hundred. 'Of course,' he said. 'Take all the time you need. Just ring me when you're ready to commit.'

11
Death List

I n the cold light of a tube train home I came to my senses.
How could I possibly go back to Roman London? I
was just a kid in Year Eight with a pathetic smattering of
Latin words.

Unlike Martin, I had no idea how to milk a goat or make
a fire. I probably wouldn't last an hour.

I pulled a small notebook out of my back pocket and
flipped it open to my list.

Ways to Die in Londinium.
1. Death by illness (no antibiotics)
2. Death by infected cut (no antiseptic cream)
3. Death by chariot (hit and run)
4. Death by starvation
5. Death by choking (no Heimlich manoeuvre)
6. Death by fire (or inhaling smoke)

7. Death by rabid animal bite

8. Death by mugger

9. Death by rampaging gladiator

10. Death by misunderstood gesture

11. Death by transporting into something solid

I dug out my pencil stub and wrote: *12. Death by Angry Priest of Mithras.*

I sighed again. Knowing my luck, I would probably die of an infected stubbed toe. Yes, Gran would get ten million pounds, but I was pretty sure she'd rather have me. Especially as I was her only grandchild.

I stuck the notebook back in my pocket and thought of what to tell her when I got home. I couldn't eat anything until after I got back from my trip to the past. Although I was starving I would have to lie and tell her I didn't feel hungry. But she might be suspicious.

She had already asked why I had gone out on Saturday lunchtime and Tuesday evening. I told her the truth, part of it. That it was to improve my Latin. And I also told her we were going on a Latin-club trip to Bath Spa from Friday to Sunday. It helped that Miss Okonmah had sent an official-looking slip home for Gran to sign. But if I told her I wasn't hungry she might think I was ill and she might not let me go on the 'Latin-club trip'.

Today was Wednesday. If I wanted to go, I just had to

get through tonight and tomorrow without eating. Then I would be empty enough to go on Friday morning.

I stopped by the dead Christmas trees near the entrance to our stairwell. Had it really been less than a week since I had been called to the headteacher's office? It seemed more like a month.

'Who am I kidding?' I muttered. 'I won't last a day in Roman London. Especially if I have to go naked and starving. What was I thinking?'

I took out my new smartphone. What had Solomon Daisy said?

If you decide to audition for the gig, then the phone is yours to keep.

I had passed the audition, so now the phone was most definitely mine.

'Just be happy with this,' I said out loud. 'You've got a cool new phone, with a year's prepaid contract, unlimited data and a hundred and twenty-eight gigabytes of storage.'

'No, you don't,' said a voice behind me. 'I do.'

And as easily as taking candy from a baby, Dinu Balan stole my smartphone.

12
Crisp-Mugger

Dinu Balan was the new boy at our school. I was new too, because I started in September, but he arrived from Romania just before Christmas, so he was officially the newest. And the biggest. For some reason he had chosen me as his favourite target. Maybe because he sat near me. Or maybe because we both get dragged along to the same church every Sunday. It's the Greek Orthodox church in Battersea, south London. The Church of St Nektarios, patron saint of bees. I bet you've never heard of him before.

Every day at break time he steals my crisps.

Not Saint Nektarios.

Dinu.

You'd think I would learn not to bring a packet of crisps every day, but I love salt-and-vinegar crisps almost more than life itself, and deep down I'm an optimist. I live in hope.

However, this was the first time he had mugged me for

49

more than crisps. He popped up in front of me with that big dumb grin, plucked the phone out of my startled hand and then scarpered.

I looked after him in dismay.

Sure, I could have chased him. But I'm a fast runner. I might have caught up with him. Then what?

I couldn't go to the police because then my gran would ask where I got the phone in the first place and I had been sworn to secrecy about my mission.

That's what decided it for me.

'I'm going to do it!' I told myself. 'I'm going back in time.'

Then, with the million pounds payable upon successful completion of the mission – five mil if I found the girl – I could buy a hundred thousand smartphones.

I could also buy my gran a proper house, not just a flat. And I could go to a posh private school with fourteen kids per class instead of thirty-two. And no bullies. A school where I could do drama and Latin and maybe even ancient Greek.

As I came up the stairs I could smell the wonderful aroma of thyme, tomato and slow-cooked sausage. Gran was cooking one of my favourite dishes: *gigantes*, also known as giant beans.

It was pure torture.

My stomach rumbled but I knew I would have to make up a story about feeling queasy. The sooner I went, the sooner I could get the cash and the sooner Gran and I could move to somewhere better.

I'm not saying our flat was a dump or anything. But my bedroom was hardly bigger than a cupboard. Also, Gran and I have to share a bathroom. She has all her candles and essential oils in there.

Gran was a hippy in her younger days and she still loves all that Age of Aquarius stuff. Our flat is decorated with faded Turkish carpets and batik wall hangings and potted ferns with macramé webbing and fringed Paisley scarves hung over lamps to make colourful lights on the wall and ceiling. (I think I'm the only kid at school who knows what 'batik', 'macramé' and 'Paisley' mean.) Gran often burns joss sticks and sometimes she lights all the candles in the house and puts on music by rock groups with strange names like Jefferson Airplane or Canned Heat. Other times she plays Greek pop songs from the sixties and once a month we have to do the Zorba dance.

But she is a great cook. It took all my will power to tell her I felt a bit off and was going to skip dinner.

It turned out she wasn't feeling too well either, so we both went to bed early. But my empty stomach wouldn't let me sleep. I tried reciting the mantra 'Five million pounds' over and over.

But that didn't help, so I fired up my laptop, an ancient MacBook Pro. Its software is long out of date, but it can still access the Internet. I did some research on fasting. Most people agreed that the first two days are the hardest and then you get a kind of Zen calm and find you have more energy and clarity of thinking.

I just needed to last one more day before the Zen calm kicked in.

Then on Friday morning I could go to the Mithraeum and travel back to the past. Solomon Daisy didn't want me to stay more that forty-eight hours, so that meant I would be back by Sunday. Trying not to think about Martin's foot and all the other things that could go wrong, I kept reciting my five-million-pounds mantra.

At last I fell asleep.

That night I dreamed I was fighting a man with a bird's head in a giant sandpit.

I was pretty sure that wasn't a good omen.

And as you will see, I was right.

13
Time Bubble

My gran loves me, which is why every Sunday she takes me hostage. I'm not allowed to go on my computer. If I had a smartphone, I wouldn't be able to go on that either. She calls it 'Culture Sunday'.

We have to go to church in the morning. Like I said, it's the Church of St Nektarios in Battersea. If there's a blizzard outside or her back is acting up then we do our own church service at home and play backgammon or cards after lunch. But on her good days the 'culture' part comes after church when she drags me to a museum or a play.

One Sunday afternoon in the summer we went to an art gallery by the River Thames called Tate Modern. We were there to see an exhibition of pop art. I thought it would be boring, but it was actually quite good. One artist had made paintings that looked like of comic-book panels and another — a sculptor — made massive balloon animals out of plastic.

Anyway, the point of this story is the soap bubbles.

Outside the museum on the public walkway overlooking the river was a man with a big soap-bubble maker. It was just two sticks with a loop of rope strung between them. He dipped it into an inflatable kiddy pool of soapy water, then lifted the loop using the two sticks. Whenever he waved it, ginormous soap bubbles floated up and along the walkway or away over the water. I'm not sure how he made any money out of his giant soap bubbles. Maybe if you paid him you got to have a go.

The reason I mention him is because that's what the time portal looked like. A giant soap-bubble maker. It was a

circular ring of plastic covered with a film of shimmering light like a soap bubble.

It was just before eight o'clock on Friday morning and I was standing in the nave of London Mithraeum with Solomon Daisy and his two tech guys. Miss Okonmah from school was there too, which surprised me. I was wearing nothing but a paper hospital gown and paper slippers. And I was looking at a giant soap bubble.

Only when I looked closer I saw it wasn't liquid. It was flame. Like the flames on Gran's gas hob.

'I have to go through *that*?' I said. 'It looks like magic fire.'

'*Non magia, sed scientia*,' said Solomon Daisy. 'It's not magic; it's science. But it is a kind of fire,' he added. 'It will burn away some of the external bacteria and parasites.'

'Parasites? You mean like fleas and ticks and worms? I don't have any of those . . .'

'Of course you do. Everybody does. Did you know you have tiny mites living in your eyebrows and eyelashes?'

'Yuck,' I said. And then, 'Won't it burn me too?'

'Not if you go through fast. You know that party trick where you pass your finger through the flame of a candle?'

'No,' I said. 'I do not know of a party trick where you hold your finger in a flame. It sounds stupid.'

'I suppose it is a bit stupid,' he said. 'But if you pass your finger through a small flame real quick it doesn't burn. Well, not too quick. But quick.'

'So I have to go through quick but not too quick?'

'Exactly.'

'Your scientific accuracy fills me with confidence,' I said.

He ignored my sarcasm. 'Have you ever been on a roller coaster?' he said.

'Once. When I was about seven or maybe eight. I hated it.'

'Well, this will be like going through a flame on a roller coaster. Also, prepare for the ground level to be a little lower. So it will be like going down a step.'

'What if I twist my ankle. Or break it?'

'Then come back through the portal immediately. But remember to come back around to the front. It only goes one way, like a revolving door. And if something goes wrong you must come back right away. We turn the portal off after five minutes and will then only turn it on for five minutes every twelve hours. By the way,' he added, 'meet my tech guys, Jeff with a J and Geoff with a G.'

I looked at his technicians. They were two guys in jeans and T-shirts. Jeff with a J was a skinny Asian-looking dude with glasses. Geoff with a G had ginger hair and a little matching beard. They both held portable consoles that looked worryingly like the controls of an Xbox.

They did not fill me with confidence.

Suddenly I felt sick, like my stomach was full of flapping pigeons.

'What if I decide not to go through?'

'If you don't want to do it,' said Miss Okonmah, 'then don't.'

She looked at Solomon Daisy and raised her eyebrows.

'Of course you don't have to go through,' said Solomon Daisy, 'even though you did sign a contract.' Then he forced a smile. 'Don't worry, Alex. It's going to be cool and you're going to be great. You're going to go back in time! Just repeat the mantra *"One million pounds to go back, five if I find the girl with the ivory knife."*'

'Yeah, I've been thinking about that too,' I said. 'What if the knife wasn't hers?'

'What do you mean?' asked Solomon Daisy.

I looked down at my paper slippers and took a deep breath. 'When I was nine, my parents were killed in a car crash. My mum was cremated but my gran – my dad's mum – wanted him buried. My grief counsellor told Gran it would be good for me to see him in his coffin. I put my favourite teddy bear in with him so he wouldn't be lonely.' I looked up at Solomon Daisy. 'What if the knife didn't belong to the girl with the blue eyes? What if it belonged to somebody else? Like maybe her dad?'

Solomon Daisy nodded slowly. 'That's a very good point,' he said, 'but I'm positive the knife is hers.'

'How?'

'Remember I told you I was obsessed with her and that I once had a vivid dream about her?'

'Yes,' I said.

'Well, in my dream she was wearing the ivory knife on her belt. I think it's her lucky talisman.'

I stared at him.

Yup, I thought. *Solomon Daisy is crazy all right. Crazier than a jar of rainbow-coloured weasels. And I am putting my life in his hands.*

14
Million-Pound Mantra

'You might think I'm crazy,' Solomon Daisy went on, 'but I know the knife is hers. So once again, repeat after me: *"Five million pounds if I find the girl with the ivory knife."*'

I nodded and took a deep breath. *'Five million pounds,'* I said, *'if I find the girl with the ivory knife.'* The flapping pigeons in my stomach felt more like butterflies now. 'Remind me how I get back?' I asked Solomon Daisy.

'Once you've gone through, we'll wait five minutes or so in case you need to come straight back. But then we have to turn it off to let it recharge. Every twelve hours we'll turn it on again for five minutes and you can come back then.' He looked at his watch. 'It's just gone eight o'clock.'

'Is eight o'clock our time the same as eight o'clock their time?'

'Almost certainly not. But you can calculate. Whatever time it is when you arrive, come back through twelve hours later or twenty-four hours later, or thirty-six, but no more than forty-eight. You get the idea.'

'Why no more than forty-eight?'

'It will take four years off your life expectancy. And you'll start to feel weak from fasting.'

'And what happens if there are tourists here in the Mithraeum when I come back naked?'

'The Mithraeum is open to the public between ten and five. We turn on the portal for five minutes at eight in the morning and again at eight at night, well outside opening hours.'

'I won't have a watch. How will I tell what time it is?'

'Our inner time clock is better than you think. Be there ready a little earlier if you're in doubt.'

'Just remember to enter through the same side as you went out,' said Jeff the Asian tech guy. 'It's counterintuitive.'

'What if someone from the past accidentally comes through?' I said. 'Like a priest of Mithras or an enraged bull?'

'Only someone who's been through can return,' said Geoff the ginger tech guy.

'We think,' said Jeff with a J.

Solomon Daisy said, 'Anybody else will probably feel strange if they get close to it. It's likely that they'll avoid the spot.'

'That's another reason why we only turn it on for five minutes at a time,' said Geoff with a G, 'to reduce the chances of anybody coming through by accident. You've got a five-minute time window.'

'It worked before,' said Solomon Daisy, 'with Martin.'

'Apart from him losing one of his feet,' I muttered. The flapping pigeons in my stomach were back, so I mentally chanted my mantra: *'Five million pounds if I find the girl with the ivory knife.'*

Solomon Daisy clapped his meaty hands and then rubbed them together. 'I've got a good feeling about this, Alex,' he said. 'Now, one more time – what are the three rules?'

I closed my eyes and recited them: *'Naked I go and naked I return. Drink, don't eat. As little interaction as possible.'* I felt a bit dizzy and had to sit down on the low wall to the right of the nave.

'Are you all right?' Daisy said.

I nodded. 'Just hungry, I guess.'

He patted my back. 'You'll be fine.'

I stood up. In just paper slippers and gown, more than my feet were beginning to feel cold. I had goosebumps all over.

I took a step forward. I was about an arm's length from the shimmery film of flame when all the little hairs on my arm and neck lifted up.

'I can feel it,' I said.

'Good,' said Solomon Daisy. He looked at the technicians. 'Ready, guys?'

They looked at their consoles and then each nodded at him.

'All right,' said Solomon Daisy. 'The moment has come. Take off your slippers and gown and give them to me.'

I glanced at Miss Okonmah, the headteacher at my school.

'Don't worry, Alex,' she said. 'I'm here for your protection.' She smiled. 'But if you're feeling shy, I'll turn around.'

'Yes, please,' I said. And recited, *'Five million pounds if I find the girl with the ivory knife.'*

After Miss Okonmah turned around, I stripped off and stood shivering in the murky darkness of London's Mithraeum, protecting my modesty with my hands.

'Good luck and off you go!' cried Solomon Daisy.

I formed a quick prayer in my head and took a deep breath. Then, reminding myself to be quick but not too quick, I stepped through the soap-bubble portal of flame.

15
Travel Sic

Solomon Daisy had told me that going through the portal would be like a roller-coaster ride.

He was wrong.

First of all, I had forgotten there would be a step down. When the ground wasn't where I expected it to be I fell forward, landing hard on my hands and knees. For a long moment I couldn't breathe. Then at last my lungs remembered what to do and sucked in air. But the air was different. Colder. Damper. With a hint of burnt pine.

My body was fizzing inside and out. I could hear a high-pitched ringing in my ears. It felt less like a bad roller-coaster ride and more like I imagined 'the bends', that thing scuba divers get if they come up too fast.

As if the tingling on my skin and the squealing in my ears and the damp in my nose weren't bad enough, my eyes were glued shut like after a long sleep.

When I managed to prise them open I felt a jolt of panic. I was blind.

They had sent me into the past naked as a newborn and blind as a bat!

Then I understood. It was dark because I was in a temple with no windows, designed to resemble a cave. As my eyes adjusted, I realised it wasn't pitch black but dark green, like being deep underwater. Straight ahead I could just make out the statue of a man in a floppy hat sitting on a bull.

It had worked! Solomon Daisy had sent me back to the Temple of Mithras, presumably in the year 260 AD or thereabouts. The tingling in my arms and legs was calming down and the ringing in my ears was beginning to fade.

Feeling dizzy, I got slowly to my feet and turned to find the source of the eerie green light. It was the circular portal, with its filmy bubble skin. In a pitch-black setting it actually gave off a faint light.

Suddenly, the green exploded in a blinding flash as a shape leaped towards me. I jumped back, tripped on a step leading up to the statue and sat down hard.

The green flash faded, leaving me in darkness again. In my ears, a strange moaning noise overlaid the fading bat-squeal.

'Oh,' moaned a voice.

Someone had come through the portal after me!

'Oh!' came the moan again. And then a voice with a Romanian accent said, 'Wimpy? Are you here?'

I could hardly believe what I was hearing.

'Dinu?' My voice came out croaky. 'Dinu, is that you?'

The only reply was the sound of someone heaving and then being violently sick. A moment later I caught a rancid whiff of vomit.

Now I wanted to be sick too, but I had nothing in my stomach to throw up.

'Dinu, what are you doing here?' My voice was still croaky.

The flash of green had temporarily blinded me, but now my eyes were readjusting. Silhouetted against the green portal I saw the shape of a boy on hands and knees.

'I saw you go through naked, so I did too,' he said. 'They tried to stop me but they weren't fast enough.' He started laughing and finished up vomiting again.

'You idiot! You're not supposed to eat for two days beforehand,' I said. 'You could have killed us both. If I hadn't crawled away you could have materialised inside me and we'd both be dead!'

'Oh!' This time it was a whimper.

My anger actually made me feel a little better. Then a thought hit me like a number forty-four bus. 'Dinu, do you have any fillings in your teeth?'

'No.' It came out as a moan. 'Why?'

'Because if you'd had anything inorganic in your body, you'd have exploded like a cat in a microwave.'

'What is inorganic?'

'It means metal or stone or anything not alive.'

'Oh!' he moaned again.

'Dinu,' I said, 'do you even know where we are?'

'Another dimension? Like TV show *Stargate*? Maybe another planet?'

'No. This is a time portal. We've gone back in time nearly two thousand years.'

'To time of cavemen?'

'No, you idiot! To Roman London.'

'Oh!' He retched again.

The stink of vomit filled my head. I tried to breathe through my mouth instead of my nose.

'Dinu, go back now.'

'Yeah. I think you right maybe,' he said. 'I don't feel so good. But how?'

'Can you see a circle of faintly glowing green light?'

There was a pause and then, 'No.'

'You can't see that greenish light?'

'My eyelids are stuck together.'

'Open them!'

'I can't.'

'Wait. I'll guide you.'

I took a step forward and almost slipped in something warm and slimy and wet.

'Ugh!' I drew my bare foot back and moved a little to the side.

'Wimpy, where are you?' he moaned.

A moment later I grasped his arm. 'Got you!' I said.

He replied by vomiting.

'Ugh!' I said. Then, 'Hurry. We have to go back around to the front of the portal. I'll push you through. You've got to go up a bit, like the first step of stairs. Good. But not there. Here. It's right here. Now go!'

But at the very moment I gave him a shove, the hum stopped and the light faded. Dinu took several stumbling steps forward and bashed into the big statue of Mithras on the bull.

'Ow!' he said.

'Oh no!' I groaned. 'I don't believe it!'

I was stuck in the past with my arch-nemesis for at least another twelve hours.

16
Wimpy Tarzan

In the dark space of the Mithraeum, Dinu the class bully was still vomiting.

I cursed in Greek, using a word my gran had told me never to say.

'Listen, Dinu,' I said when he finally stopped, 'I've got a mission here in Roman London, but you don't have a clue. In fact, you could ruin everything.'

'You have mission?' he said.

'Yes. And hopefully it won't take more than two days. So why don't you just wait here? When you feel that hum again and see the greenish light, step through. It will be in about twelve hours. There should be a well with water in it just over there.'

'No.' He grabbed my arm. 'I'll go with you. I want treasure too.'

I groaned. 'I'm not looking for treasure, Dinu. I'm looking

for a person. I've got to find a blue-eyed girl with an ivory leopard knife. That's all.'

'A girl?'

'A girl.'

'No treasure?'

'The only treasure I'll get is a reward from that big guy you might have seen as you followed me through the portal. How did you get in anyway?'

'They left the door open.' He retched again.

I took a deep breath. 'Listen – you've got to wait here. It's a kind of ancient temple. If men come in to do their ceremony, just hide behind the bull statue and keep quiet, OK? And if you hear a hum and see a green soap-bubble thing, then come around this side and step through. But don't wear any clothes or take anything.'

'No,' came his voice. 'I will not stay alone.'

'Dinu. You haven't prepared. You don't know a word of Latin. You might ruin everything. You might even change the future.'

His hand gripped my wrist even harder. 'No. Take me with you. Please.'

I felt dizzy and had to sit on the side of the nave. The columns were real and solid. I leaned against one.

When my dizzy spell passed, I said, 'All right. You can come with me on a couple of conditions.'

'Yes. You name them.'

'First, let go of my wrist. You're cutting off my blood supply.'

He let go of my wrist.

'If you want to come with me,' I said, 'you have to promise to stick with me, obey my every command and not say a word. In fact, you have to pretend to be my slave.'

'I promise.'

'Really?'

'Really.'

'Swear it.'

Dinu said, 'I swear I will pretend to be your slave. I will do everything you say. I will not say a word.'

Then he expelled something through his other portal.

'Ugh!' I groaned as I caught the smell. After a while I said, 'Finished?'

'I think.' He sounded miserable.

'OK. Then let's get out of here. Are your eyes open now?'

'Not sure. I can only see grey and black.'

'That's because we're in a temple designed to resemble a cave. Can you see me waving my arm?'

I waved my arm slowly.

'Yes.'

'Good. Then follow me.'

I led the way down the nave towards the entrance. The floor was made of smooth oak planks. Dim light showed columns looming on either side but wasn't bright enough to prevent me from stubbing my toe on a small block of stone, possibly an altar. I cursed in Greek and moved into the centre of the nave.

'Come on,' I said. 'The exit should be this way.'

A soft moan behind me was the only reply.

Then I saw a faint thread of light up ahead. It outlined double doors at a higher level. My cautious toes found a step, then another, then another.

'Ow!' yelped Dinu.

'Watch out for the stairs,' I said.

When I reached the double doors my groping fingers found a crossbar and I managed to lift it up. According to Martin, beyond these doors was an anteroom leading to a changing room for priests where I would find water and clothes.

The inner double doors opened with a squeak and I saw the anteroom. Small high windows let in a little light and showed another set of double doors straight ahead and also a small wooden door on my left.

Going through the small door brought me into the brightest room yet. It had a vaulted ceiling and two high unglazed windows. A kind of shelf bench covered with the same grey plaster as the walls ran around three sides of the room. The floor was concrete and sloped down to a small bowl-shaped marble drain with four comma-shaped holes in it. I spotted a well in the far corner, and when I came closer I could see a mop in a wooden bucket next to it.

This must be the changing room for the priests of Mithras. But where were the robes? Apart from the bucket and mop, the room was totally empty.

Approaching the wooden bucket, I saw that the mop was just a wooden stick with a short bar at the end wrapped in a rag. I gingerly picked it up and the rag came away. It was loosely woven and damp, and barely big enough to tie around my waist, but it was better than nothing.

You know Tarzan, that guy who swings through the jungle on vines, wearing a tiny animal-skin loincloth?

I looked like a wimpy Tarzan, but at least my modesty was covered.

'What about me?' said a voice from the doorway.

I turned to see more of Dinu Balan than I ever hoped or expected. I couldn't help but feel sorry for the bully who had mugged me for my crisps the past few weeks. His face was a chalky white, his chest covered with yellow vomit and his legs streaked with brown.

'Come and stand here,' I said, pointing at the drain in the floor. I looked into the well and saw another bucket, this one leather. It was attached to a wooden dowel by a rope and could be lowered or raised by turning a wooden crank. I let the bucket down into the well and cranked it up again. The water in it looked clear enough so I took a sip. It tasted slightly musty but I was thirsty so I drank deeply. *Rule number two: Drink, don't eat.*

I rinsed Dinu's vomit off my feet. The water was ice cold.

'Crouch down a little and close your eyes,' I said.

Dinu dutifully bent forward and rested his hands on his knees. I brought the bucket as close to him as the rope would allow.

Then I emptied it over him.

'Aaaargh! Is freezing!' I ignored his protests and sluiced him down three more times. I even made him turn around and bend over. That is a sight I will never unsee.

At last he stood shivering and naked. His blond hair was plastered to his wide forehead, making him look like a drowned rat, but a clean drowned rat at least.

'Are you ready?' I said. 'Stay close to me and don't say anything, all right?'

Dinu nodded meekly and used the wooden bucket to cover his groin. I had to turn quickly so he wouldn't see my smile.

Who cared about Roman London and the blue-eyed girl from Africa with the ivory leopard knife? It was worth the misery to get a little revenge on Dinu Balan.

I went out of the changing room and back into the dimly lit anteroom between the two sets of double doors. The doors leading to the outside were barred, but for anyone inside that posed no problem. I lifted the wooden plank from its cradle, pushed the doors, and stepped out into the past.

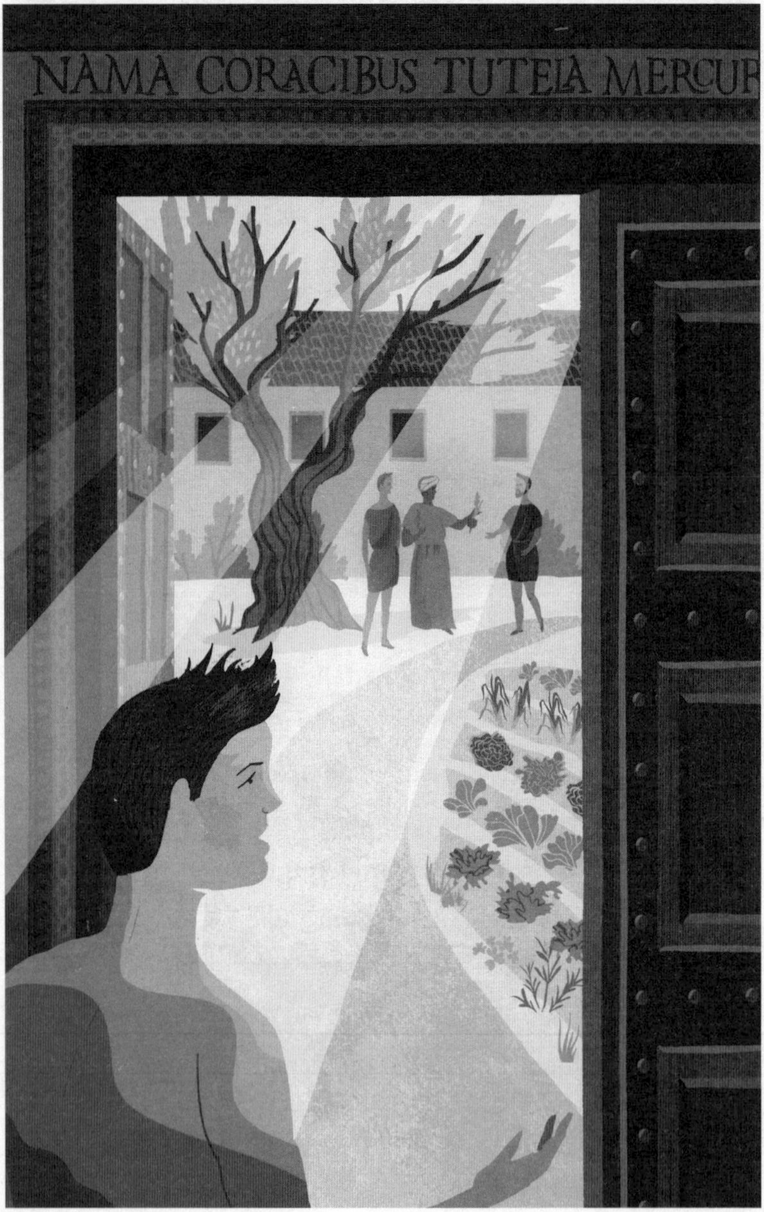
NAMA CORACIBUS TUTELA MERCUR

17
Roman T-Shirts

Have you ever had that nightmare where you show up at school to find everybody pointing at you and laughing and you realise you're wearing only your Spiderman underwear?

That's what it was like when I first stepped out of the Mithraeum in my Tarzan loincloth. I'd been told that the temple was in the garden of a private villa.

So I wasn't expecting an audience.

Outside, the soft light of a summer evening showed what looked like a big vegetable garden. A single tall tree grew in its centre, and standing beneath this tree I saw three men. One – a stocky guy – wore something like an orange bathrobe and a matching turban. The other two were skinny and wore long pale blue T-shirts.

No. Not T-shirts.

Tunics.

They were ancient Romans and I was in Londinium!

I only had a moment to take all this in. They had been examining something – a large turnip, I think – and were already turning to look at me.

For a moment we gawped at each other.

Then the guy in orange pointed. First he shouted, '*Heus!*', the Latin version of 'Oi! You!' Then he bellowed something that sounded like '*Captem!*' I didn't need to understand Latin to know he meant, 'Get him!'

I turned to look at Dinu. He stood unmoving, the wooden bucket covering his private parts and his eyes wide with astonishment.

The two skinny guys in blue tunics started running towards us.

'Come on, Dinu!' I muttered under my breath. 'Run!'

Without waiting to see if he would follow, I charged around the corner and raced down a muddy path that ran between the outer wall of the Mithraeum and a cane-fenced garden. My plan had always been to go along the north side of the temple to the stream called Walbrook and follow it down to the Thames. Then I would cross over the original London Bridge and make my way to the urine-scented fullers', so that I could find Caecilius the knife-seller who might be able to point me to the blue-eyed girl from Africa.

Now I was running with the Mithraeum on my left and an

allotment on my right. It looked just like the vegetable patch out of Peter Rabbit. It must have rained recently because the long grass at the edge of the path made my legs wet.

'*Furcifer!*' shouted one of the slaves in pursuit.

I almost laughed out loud. *Furcifer* was one of the first words we had learned in Latin club. It means 'scoundrel' or 'crook'.

I risked a look over my shoulder – Dinu was about two paces behind me and our two skinny pursuers were not far behind him.

When I turned back I saw a white head with evil yellow eyes and horns rising up above the tall grass straight ahead. A goat!

I veered right to avoid it, but Dinu hadn't seen it. He took a spectacular tumble and ended up flat on his back.

He was up in a second, without his bucket, and running free.

But now the angry goat was aiming his horns at our pursuers and they slowed down.

Just ahead on my right I spied three pale blue tunics draped over a kind of trellis that formed the far end of the garden fence. I grabbed one and pulled it over my head with a prayer of thanks to the God I hadn't known till now that I believed in. The tunic was too big and faintly damp, but I didn't mind. Dinu tried to follow my example and nab another tunic, but it caught on one of the slats of cane that made up the fence. He managed to tug it off, but nearly pulled the whole fence down.

A small part of me thought it strange that they would leave clothes drying on the fence like that, with no wall to protect them from robbers. Then I stepped out into empty space, and in the split second before I hit the water I remembered why they didn't need a wall to protect the west side of the garden.

They had a perfectly good stream.

18
Bog Kid

When I say the Walbrook was 'a perfectly good stream', I mean it was good as a boundary that no sane person would ever cross.

The real version didn't have creepy tree roots like the bronze sculpture outside twenty-first-century Bloomberg Arcade. It was much deeper, freezing cold and with unmentionable things floating in it.

There was a huge splash behind me and I managed to turn and see Dinu doing the doggy paddle. Up on the bank, our two pursuers were shaking their fists and still crying, 'Furcifer!'

They seemed unwilling to follow us in.

Maybe they couldn't swim.

Of course they couldn't swim.

There were no swimming pools in Londinium apart from maybe a hot plunge in the baths.

And you don't need to know how to swim to take a bath.

Also, nobody in his right mind would want to swim in this brook. I could not imagine anything worse.

Then I was swept into the Thames.

It was even colder than the Walbrook, and just as full of floating things, but with the added element of being much more dangerous because there were boats everywhere. My head nearly struck one the size of a bathtub made of leather. What was that kind of boat called? A barnacle? No: a coracle.

'Help!' I made a swipe for it, but already I was being whirled past it and the open-mouthed face of the boy inside.

When I turned away, I realised the current wanted to slam me into a big wooden ship up ahead. I thrashed with my arms and kicked with my feet and only just managed not to get my brains bashed out by a giant paddle.

I knew I had to get to the south side of the river, but I had got turned around and no longer knew which way was which. Plus this ancient version of the Thames seemed twice as wide as the river I knew.

Then I glimpsed a big wooden bridge between two boats. I knew Londinium had only one bridge across the Thames, and it was east of the Walbrook.

I struck out for what I hoped was the south bank.

My legs and arms felt as if a thousand freezing needles were pricking them. A couple of times I gulped water instead of air.

I tried not to think about what else I might have swallowed.

Finally, just when I thought I couldn't swim any further, I realised the water wasn't tugging at me as much as before. I managed to float on my back for a moment and gather my thoughts.

Dinu! Where was he?

I trod water and looked around, but couldn't spot him among the flotilla of boats.

'Dinu!' I shouted, but only got a mouthful of water.

So I turned and paddled for shore.

I almost sobbed with relief as my numb toes felt slippery mud and soon I was staggering out of the water. The sun was low in the sky, making an angry orange smear. It was setting on my right, which probably meant I had made it to the south bank.

But you can never tell with the Thames; it curves like a snake.

Finally I was out of the water and wading through grey mud. But I wasn't home free. In fact, it was getting harder and harder to move. Every time I pulled my leg out it was covered with more mud than before. And with every step I sank deeper. After about five more minutes of this, I found myself stuck up to my waist. I squirmed and writhed but only managed to wedge myself tighter.

There was something evil about the cold and slippery grey mud, like it wanted to suck me down. My heart was pounding so hard that I felt sick. I took deep breaths and tried to think what to do.

Once when I was in Year Four, the Thames River Police came to our school and told us never to go down on the foreshore without supervision. A few weeks before, three teenagers from Putney had taken a boat for a midnight joyride. Out near Hammersmith they had seen a kind of island in the river and got out of the boat to explore. Then they started to sink into the mud.

'We rescued two of them but there was still one missing,' said the policeman. 'It was a dark night and we were shining our torches and powerful floodlights. We were about to give up when the beam showed us a little patch of white. It was the girl's cheek. She was up to her neck in the mud. We were just in time. A few more minutes and she would have been gone forever.'

After the police left, our teacher, Mr Rowley, showed us a photo of the famous Bog Man, a guy who died in a muddy bog in Denmark about three thousand years ago and got preserved like a mummy.

I thought of my list.

Of all the ways to die in Londinium, being drowned in the evil grey mud of the River Thames had not occurred to me.

But it seemed that was to be my fate.

I was going to end up as Bog Kid.

19
Mud Woman

If you have a fairly good memory for words and can imitate Yoda from *Star Wars*, then you can probably speak Latin. The trick is to put the verb at the end.

Powerful you have become.

Patience you must have.

When nine hundred years you reach, look as good you will not.

My first proper Latin sentence to a proper Roman Londoner was, '*Gratias ago.*'

Thanks I give.

Or 'Thank you.'

I said it to the woman who was coming to pull me out of the mud and save me from a sticky death. Dressed in a brown sack with holes poked in it for her head and arms, she clomped towards me across the mud like Frankenstein's monster. On her feet were strange shoes that looked like tennis racquets made of strips of wood and tied with leather thongs. They weren't snowshoes; they were mud-shoes. That's why she was able to walk out on the marshy foreshore to help me.

She had dirt-brown dreadlocks, a toothless mouth and crusted streaks of mud on her face. Her arms were scrawny but surprisingly strong as she grabbed me beneath my underarms and tugged.

I tried not to giggle and finally came out with a sucking sound and lay flat on my back on the mud. I must have looked like a Magnum bar, only coated with grey mud rather than chocolate.

'*Thank you,*' I said again in Latin.

In reply she grabbed my tunic and tried to tug it over my head.

I was trying to think how to say, 'That's very kind of you, but I can wash it later, once I'm on dry ground,' when I realised she wasn't trying to help me.

She was trying to rob me of my tunic.

I couldn't really be offended. After all, I had just stolen it from the Mithraeum villa. But that didn't mean I was going to let her have it.

I sat up and pushed her away.

That was when she unlooped the wooden-handled knife hanging from a tattered rope belt around her waist.

In a hoarse voice she said something that I didn't understand, but the way she was brandishing the knife made it crystal clear what she wanted.

'*Nego!*' I shouted. It was the only word I could think of in my panic. It literally means 'I say no, deny or refuse', and probably was the ancient equivalent of 'I should think not!'

'*Furcifer!*' she growled, and thrust the knife at me.

If I hadn't been so skinny she would have got me. But I managed to roll to one side and she only put the dagger through my mud-encrusted tunic.

A surge of adrenaline gave me strength to grab her bony wrist and twist it until she screeched in pain and dropped the knife. I tossed it over her head and shoved her onto her back.

'*Furcifer!*' she screamed at me. '*Furcifer!*'

Ignoring her screams, I pulled off her mud-shoes, slipped my gooey feet into them and began to stagger towards drier land.

I didn't make very good time because I hadn't done the laces of the mud-shoes properly and they were clumsy. Also, my muddy tunic kept flapping between my legs. When I reached the knife, I picked it up. No point making it easy for her to try to stick me again.

When I thought it was safe, I looked back.

I almost screamed.

The woman was only a few metres behind me, crawling on her belly and using her elbows to drag herself forward. Behind her a snail-trail of water reflected the red sunset and looked like blood. She was a terrifying sight.

20
Mini-Volcanoes

In my panic to get away from the woman I tripped over one of the mud-shoes and it came off. I had to sit and put down the knife so that I could tie it on. My fingers were slippery and clumsy. At last I managed to tie the thong. I rose unsteadily to my feet just as she reached me. We both lunged for the knife, but I got it first and squelched away as fast as I could.

Looking back, I saw her still lying where I had left her. She was shaking her fist at me, but I could tell she was exhausted. I almost felt sorry for her and as soon as I reached relatively dry land, I took off the mud-shoes and held them up to show I was leaving them for her.

I wasn't leaving her the knife though. That might come in handy.

I shaded my eyes against the last rays of the setting sun. No sign of Dinu.

I feared the worst.

Looking further inland, I saw some low mud-and-thatch huts on my right and some clay beehive-shaped things on my left with smoke coming up from some of them. Beyond them was more smoke, a kind of low-lying smog.

That must be Londinium, or rather Southwark.

That was where the blue-eyed girl had been buried and probably lived too.

That was the way I needed to go. The only problem was that the path to the beehive structures was blocked by two people coming towards me: a little man with a wispy beard and a boy about my size. The boy's eyes were red and swollen, which made him look a bit like a pig. They both wore loincloths a bit like the Tarzan mop-rag I had on underneath my tunic.

It seemed that decent clothes were hard to come by in Londinium.

As they got closer I could see from their angry expressions that they weren't coming to help me.

I waved my knife at them and shouted, '*Desiste!*'

They stopped and frowned at each other. Later I realised I'd used the singular imperative as if I only wanted one of them to stop. Maybe they had been confused. Or maybe they were as frightened of me as I was of them. After all, I had a knife and they didn't. Now barefoot, I ran straight towards them and they jumped aside, staring at me wide-eyed.

I kept going across the scrubby ground towards the beehive buildings, only stopping when I nearly fell into a big round pit filled with water. I saw a wooden ramp going into it and noticed chunks cut out of the grey mud. It was a kind of clay quarry. Maybe they were making pots. Or roof tiles.

The thick mud was drying on my legs and arms; I was starting to feel like the Thing, that Marvel superhero who is made of rock.

The sun had almost set and a quick glance confirmed that nobody was around so I went down the ramp and washed off as much of the mud as I could.

I came out, shivering and dripping. Now I was coated in a thin film of grey but at least I didn't look like the Thing any more. I peeked around one of the clay beehives to see if Dinu had appeared yet. He was nowhere to be seen.

But the mud woman was.

She had reached dry ground, replaced her mud-shoes and was now talking to the man and the boy and pointing towards my hiding place. They turned to look, but I shrank back out of sight. Next time I looked, all three of them were heading away from me towards the mud-and-thatch huts.

Breathing a sigh of relief, I edged around my beehive to see two skinny men in grubby tunics bending over the base of another big beehive. They were shovelling pieces of wood into a space underneath it. I could see the red glow of coals inside.

It must be a kiln, for baking pots. Thankfully, the men didn't notice me as I backed away and hid behind one of the other kilns, gratefully soaking up some of its warmth.

Up above, the first star had appeared in a dark blue sky along with a thin sliver of moon.

Leaning against the kiln, damp and barefoot, I prayed that age-old prayer.

> *Star light, star bright,*
> *First star I see tonight*
> *I wish I may, I wish I might*
> *Have the wish I wish tonight:*
> *May I survive and find the girl*
> *Return back home and get five mil.*

The sound of men's voices made me tense all my muscles, ready to run.

But it was only the kiln-slaves going away, luckily in another direction.

I realised that if anyone saw me wearing nothing but a damp slave's tunic and with a knife in one hand, they would probably assume I was a crazed runaway. They would attack first and question me later.

I badly needed a belt for my knife, but had no idea where I would find one. Then I remembered my loincloth. I put the knife on the ground, reached up under my tunic, undid the knot and pulled out the rag. Using my knife, which was disturbingly sharp, I cut the rag into three strips. I stretched them out, which was not difficult as the weave was so loose. Next I tied the strips together at one end, used my heel to anchor the knot to the ground and wove the three strips into a plait. I knotted the other end and was relieved to find this braided rag was long enough to go around my waist. Once I had tied it, I realised I could tug up my damp tunic to let a flap hang over the makeshift belt. This raised the hem of the tunic to just below my knees rather than almost to my ankles, making walking much easier. It also made a kind of pouch down the front of my tunic. For a moment I considered dropping the knife down there, but it was not a folding knife, and the razor-sharp blade might cut me.

In the end I stuck the knife between the belt and tunic. Now I felt like a Halloween pirate, but that was better than being a half-naked Tarzan.

Meanwhile, it was getting darker.

I needed somewhere safe and warm to sleep. Probably best to stay where I was. I guessed it was almost mid-summer and that it would be light again in a few hours.

So I found the warmest kiln, the one the slaves had recently stoked, and I lay on my side, curving my damp body slightly so that my thighs, belly, chest and cheek were pressed against the warm clay. The ground beneath me was baked hard as concrete, but at least it was dry. My empty stomach gurgled loudly, but I was too exhausted to take any notice. I fell asleep almost at once.

I dreamed I had gone back in time to Pompeii and was sleeping next to a mini-volcano. Then I dreamed that men were shouting questions at me and kicking me.

The mini-volcano had been in my dream.

The kicks and shouts were real.

21
Singing Stars

I was jolted awake by a kick to my ribs. A flickering torch showed me the wild-eyed faces of two men. They were painfully thin, with mangy tufts of hair on their heads. I recognised the two kiln-slaves who had been tending the fire earlier.

'*Abi!*' They were shouting. '*Abi!*'

They pointed out into the darkness.

'I'm not doing any harm,' I mumbled in English. 'It's the middle of the night. Just let me stay here till morning.'

'*Abi!*' insisted the one with the torch, and swung his foot in the direction of my ribs.

I rolled away and then pulled out my knife. That made them both jump back.

But the one with the torch kept saying, '*Abi!*' and jabbing the flaming end of his stick at me.

I pulled myself to my feet too quickly; a sudden dizziness

swept over me. I leaned against the warm cone of the kiln to steady myself.

I tried to remember the Latin phrase I had memorised.

But they only shouted, '*Abi!*' and the one without a torch gestured as if swatting a fly. I remembered Solomon Daisy's warning about misunderstanding gestures, but I was pretty certain this one meant, 'Beat it!'

I sighed and used my knife to point into the darkness. '*Londinium?*' I asked.

'*Abi!*' they repeated together. '*Abi!*'

'All right, all right,' I muttered.

Once out of the circle of torchlight, I put my knife back in my belt of plaited rag. The night was full of frogs croaking. The air was mild but damp, with a swampy smell. It was so dark that I hardly dared to move. I just stood there on waste ground, afraid of what I might step on.

After a while I sat down. There were sharp pieces of broken pottery scattered around, but I pushed them away and finally curled up on damp earth.

I longed for my own bed and my duvet or even the stupid hippy bedspread my gran had made when she was at university. I tried different positions but couldn't fall asleep. The croaking of the frogs was too loud. I heard ducks quacking too. There was also a bird with a call like a squeaky toy, maybe a coot. I never knew the night could be so noisy.

Finally I rolled onto my back and opened my eyes.

The sky was full of more stars than I had ever seen in my life.

There were a trillion of them, blazing like diamonds. I could clearly see the brighter stars that made up constellations and also a band of stars so crammed together that they formed a big curve of light, like a diamond rainbow.

I had seen the Milky Way once before, on holiday in Greece. It was impressive then, but nothing like this. This was literally awesome.

The croaking frogs seemed to be singing out the message of those stars: *We are here! The universe is vast. We are eternal.*

And I realised something. Those terrifying stars are *always there*, but we don't see them any more.

I was hypnotised.

It felt like they wanted to pull part of me into them. Like I was falling upward.

I thought, This is a dream. I'm going to wake up any minute.

But it was too real to be a dream. The swampy air was too heavy and the frogs were too loud and the stars were too bright.

What had I done? I would never find my way back and my gran wouldn't know what had happened to me and she would worry for the rest of her life.

I stared up at those stars for a long time. Eventually I must have fallen asleep, because I woke with a jerk to the sound of a mosquito whining in my ear.

The awe-inspiring stars had been replaced by a colourless pre-dawn sky. Mist blanketed the ground around me.

I sat up, rubbed sleep from my eyes. Mosquitoes were swarming around my legs. I had already been bitten several times.

I pushed myself up on my knees. Strangely, I didn't feel hungry. Just dizzy.

Then I nearly screamed. A huge hole yawned in the ground only a few paces away. Craning forward I saw that it was a rubbish pit, full of jagged shards of pottery, the corpse of a dead rat and other disgusting things. If I'd kept walking in the dark I would have fallen in and probably broken my neck.

At least I had survived the night.

I slapped at a mosquito and hoped it wasn't a malaria carrier.

It was now light enough for me to see the flat grey shapes of people and animals moving through the low mist about a stone's throw from where I sat. They were all heading in one direction. North-east, I think. Some had baskets on their backs or sacks full of goods. A few had little donkeys. A slow-moving ox-cart trundled along at the same pace as the pedestrians. It held a giant leather sack full of liquid, like an ancient tanker truck.

I stood up and waited for another wave of dizziness to

pass. Carefully going around the death pit, I picked my way through weeds and pottery shards to the road. Another ox-cart passed by, this one piled high with chopped firewood. A man in a tattered tunic had a big dog on a lead. For some reason the dog suddenly yelped and bolted. His tattered owner ran after him. A barefoot man wearing a woolly hat and something like a big nappy was driving a herd of small pigs with a stick. The pigs also seemed restless and started to squeal, so I waited for them to pass before I stepped out onto the road.

When I say 'road', I mean a kind of sticky river of mud studded with gravel. There were no trees at all, apart from a single dead one up ahead, a silhouette in the mist. To my right were marshy grasses and big puddles of water reflecting the rising sun. I noticed small tombs either side of the road and realised this must be a burial ground. Smoke was rising up from a bonfire, and as I got closer I heard music and saw about thirty men, women and children standing around it with their hands lifted.

The swirling smoke made them look like ghosts and I shuddered. They were even moaning in a spooky way, making a sound like nothing I'd ever heard. Flutes trilled and someone was shaking a tambourine or maybe some kind of rattle. It was unearthly.

Then I realised it wasn't a bonfire.

It was a dead body being burned on a pyre.

A gust of wind wafted smoke across the road and the travellers on the road started coughing. I got a noseful of it too. My empty stomach flipped as I smelled something like incense mixed with bacon.

A little firewood-laden donkey stopped and began to make an incredibly loud hee-haw noise. Its owner started beating it with a stick, but it wouldn't move.

He stood there, hitting it again and again.

I couldn't bear to watch so I hurried on, hoping to put the death and misery behind me.

Then I saw the guy on the cross.

22
Grave Concerns

The thing I had mistaken for a dead tree turned out to be a person nailed to a cross. It looked a lot like the sculpture of the crucified Jesus in church, only instead of his head being to one side it had flopped forward so – thankfully – I couldn't see his face.

It was the most horrific thing I had ever seen. Then it got worse: he moved. The poor guy was still alive!

My head was fighting with my stomach about whether to pass out or throw up, but my feet kept me moving until I was past it.

But I wasn't done with death quite yet.

Once again I heard the sound of singing, along with a flute and jingly tambourine. This music was more like a tune, and I could make out words in Latin.

It was another funeral, but these people were burying the body, not burning it. The mist parted to show me mourners and musicians on the left-hand side of the road. There were fewer of them here than at the cremation, only a dozen or so, gathered around an open grave and singing. The ones without instruments were lifting their hands and faces to the sky. Unlike the other mourners, these ones were dressed all in black or grey.

I was about to put my head down and hurry on when I had a thought. According to Solomon Daisy, the blue-eyed girl with the ivory knife had been buried in Southwark. Maybe by some fluke I had arrived on the very day of her funeral. I left the muddy road and made my way gingerly across the waste ground towards the little group of mourners. Were you allowed to gatecrash a funeral?

Apparently you were.

A few people looked at me but nobody objected.

There were ten adults and two kids standing around the grave. As I came to the grave edge, I peeped in and saw what looked like a mummy. Then I realised it was the body of a stocky woman wrapped in unbleached cloth.

I knew this from church; it was a shroud like the one they had wrapped Jesus in. Only this one wasn't bound up in strips but a kind of bag laid out on a rectangle of pure white powder, like baby powder. There was a clay cup on one side of her head and half a roast chicken on the other. I guessed she was hoping to have some food in the underworld, though how you can eat if your face is covered by a shroud I do not know.

Then someone started crying out the word *clementia*, which I think means 'mercy'.

The rest joined in. *'Clementia!'* they shouted. *'Clementia!'* Some stretched out their hands towards the body. That made me think Clementia might be the dead woman's name. One woman beat her chest and cried, *'Ai! Ai! Ai!'*

This was too intense for me, and Clementia wasn't my girl, so I backed away and returned to the path.

Up ahead, another road joined the one I was on and I saw more people with carts and pack animals.

The sun was up now, but still low in the sky. Its slanting rays made sheets of water on the marshy ground look like bronze, or maybe I should say 'copper-alloy'. Over on drier ground near the fork in the road, a statue on a column stood between two strange-looking buildings. They were both square with white columns around all four sides and smaller upper storeys poking up from their red tile roofs. I had never seen pictures of any Roman buildings that looked like that.

After a few dozen metres, I came to a low wooden bridge. Was it London Bridge? No. I had glimpsed Londinium's main bridge when I was swept out of the Walbrook. This was more like a causeway of split timbers than a proper bridge. Then I remembered Solomon Daisy telling me that some of the cemeteries were on islands surrounded by water.

I noticed that people were careful to step onto the bridge with their right foot first. Some of them lifted their hands to the sky. The man with the ox-cart tossed something into the water.

Our Latin-club teacher, Miss Forte, was always telling us that Romans believed evil spirits hung around borders and thresholds, and that if you didn't step across properly they would get you, so I also stepped onto the wooden bridge with my right foot first. I needed all the luck I could get.

I saw a heron and more ducks and some people fishing from flat-boats.

By the time I reached the middle of the bridge, I could see a few houses emerging from the mist up ahead. They were the first proper Roman London houses I'd seen.

I was surprised to see that they looked even less Roman than the two strange buildings by the fork in the road. Their walls were dirty white plaster criss-crossed with dark beams. Some even had thatched roofs.

A sudden thought froze me on the wooden bridge.

Had Crazy Daisy sent me back to the wrong period in time?

23
Demonic Dancing

Had I been sent back to medieval London or even Shakespeare's time by mistake?

The answer was revealed as the smoke thinned and I saw a very Roman-looking building.

It was made of brick and stone, and it had columns and a dome with smoke coming out. No, not smoke. Steam. It was the *mansio*, a type of Roman inn, marked on the map I had memorised.

I was being stupid. People around me were wearing tunics and hooded cloaks and they were mostly speaking Latin. Of course we were in Roman times.

I realised the strange square buildings must have been the so-called Romano-Celtic temples. I'd seen them marked on the map just before the inn and wondered what they'd look like.

'Come on, Alex!' I said to myself. 'Use your brain!'

It's just that it wasn't at all what I had imagined.

In my head I had pictured white marble columns and toga-wearing men in chariots.

So far I had seen none of these.

Instead of elegant marble temples I saw crooked buildings covered with plaster and roofed with thatch. Instead of chariots I saw rickety wagons. Instead of statues lining the road were piles of rubbish, some small and some big. Coming off the bridge, I saw that a trench ran in front of the half-timbered buildings to my left. More fires burned in metal braziers and I could smell dung, smoke and sour thatch.

Maybe Londinium would look more Roman once I was in among the shops and houses.

A grubby hen clucked across my path, pursued by a naked boy.

Female faces peeped from the unglazed windows of upper rooms.

On my right a woman sat behind a crude wooden table covered with the skulls of small animals, rodents by the look of them. She was calling out to passers-by in a voice too shrill for me to make out her words. One of the little skulls dangled from a grubby string around her neck; I guessed she was selling them as lucky charms.

The road was now less mud and more gravel, which was bad news for me. I yelped as a sharp stone hurt my right foot.

I stopped and balanced on my left foot so I could see the damage. Luckily the piece of gravel hadn't pierced the tender skin. A few other people were barefoot, but they had probably been doing it all their lives and had soles like leather.

I needed shoes.

And to get shoes I needed money.

As an ox-cart driver passed the skull-seller, she stretched out her hand and pleaded for him to buy one of her lucky skulls.

That gave me an idea.

I could beg.

I could simply sit down, hold out my hands and look pathetic. I'd seen enough of beggars in modern London to know it worked. Maybe I could even get a piece of charcoal and scribble a note on the paving stone before me: *Need shoes. Please give a coin.*

Only it would have to be in Latin. And people would have to know how to read.

I could see the awnings of market stalls up ahead, and hear the shouts of traders. Just like Northcote Road in Battersea, near where I lived.

That would be a good place to beg. I set off carefully along the side of the road near the ditch, where there was more mud and less gravel, but a sickly sweet smell made me recoil. The ditch was an open sewer. I tried to find a happy medium between the gravel road and the sewer, but had to watch out for mule pies and pig poo.

When I reached the market, I discovered that I was not the first person who had decided to beg there that morning.

Beggar Number One was a scrawny woman in a sleeveless tunic with disgusting red sores dotting her face and arms.

Beggar Number Two was a man in only a tattered loincloth, stretching out a withered hand.

Beggar Number Three was a cheerful dwarf in a pink tunic, a floppy woolly hat and multicoloured rags wrapped around his feet.

To compete with these three I would have to do something pretty impressive.

What could I do to attract people's coins? What talents did I have? Back home in the twenty-first century I could kill more zombies on the latest zombie-killing console game than anyone else in my class . . . but that wouldn't help me here.

I could juggle hacky-sacks and I could also play 'Greensleeves' on the recorder. But I had no hacky-sacks and no recorder.

I couldn't even make a giant soap bubble out of two sticks and a loop of old rope, because the Romans did not have washing-up liquid.

Maybe I could sing?

Our school's Christmas production had been *The Jungle Book* and I had been cast as Mowgli. But my favourite song was not Mowgli's but King Louie's. You know the one I mean; it's everyone's favourite.

I found an empty spot in front of a brick wall between Ragged Dwarf and a dried fish stall.

I started singing the monkey song, also known as *King of the Swingers*.

A few Roman Londoners stopped to watch and listen.

I sang it once and then started again, singing of how I wanted to be like them and stroll right into town.

A few seemed curious, most looked only blank.

Maybe it was because I was singing in English rather than Latin. If I had a day and a dictionary I might be able to translate it, but I had neither.

However I did know some jokes, the ones that every kid who learns Latin knows. So instead of singing the English words, I sang it with funny Latin ones.

'Caesar adsum iam forte!' I sang. *'Brutus aderat! Caesar sic in omnibus et Brutus sic innat.'*

It's just a bunch of Latin words that make no sense in Latin, but if you say them a certain way it sounds like 'Caesar had some jam for tea, Brutus had a rat. Caesar sick in omnibus and Brutus sick in hat.' The rhyme fit the beat of the Disney song perfectly.

The other joke Miss Forte taught us was *'Semper Ubi Sub Ubi'* which literally means 'Always Where Under Where' which sounds a bit like 'Always Wear Underwear'!

OK, I admit it: Latin is not that funny.

But singing in Latin, even in nonsense Latin, seemed

to be working. More people had stopped and were staring at me.

I needed more. In desperation, I started kicking my legs up.

'*Semper ubi sub ubi!*' I sang as I kicked my legs in time.

Two women squealed and a man in a short hooded cloak guffawed.

That was when I realised I should probably have taken heed of what I was singing: 'Always wear underwear.'

Quickly I changed tack and tried a dance popular at my school, where you swing your hips one way and your stiff arms the other real quick. Some of the boys in my class do it at break time to make the girls laugh. It's better when there are two or three of you but I was flying solo.

That dance didn't work. It was too energetic and didn't allow me to breathe, much less sing. People started to look puzzled rather than pleased.

So I tried another dance: the Carlton.

No, not the Charleston. The Carlton.

It's the dance Carlton does in *Fresh Prince of Bel Air*. It was a popular one at Wandsworth Academy.

With a big grin on my face and Carlton-style jazz hands I sang it out with gusto.

Now people looked almost scared. They must have thought I was possessed by an evil spirit or something because about half of my audience were holding up their fists with the thumb between the first and second finger, which Miss Forte had told us was the Roman sign against evil.

Yup. It seemed my dancing was demonic.

24
Choir-Boy

Disney tunes, bad Latin puns and YouTube dances were not cutting it here on the mean streets of Roman London. I remembered Miss Forte saying they had a different sense of humour in ancient times.

Yeah. Like NO SENSE OF HUMOUR.

So I decided to play it straight rather than for laughs.

Did I mention that I have a nice sweet voice? At my primary school I was often given the solo part in Christmas carols, and, like I said, I was Mowgli in *The Jungle Book*.

As I tried to think of what Latin words I could sing, I suddenly had a brainwave.

I took a deep breath and started singing my memorised phrase to the tune of 'Greensleeves'.

'*Puellam oculis caeruleis*,' I sang, '*quaero et cultro eburneo . . .*'

I had to squish some of the words together but managed to make them just about fit.

I needed a second verse so added, '*Culter eius est panthera, panthera maculata.*'

(The word *panthera* fit the rhythm better than *leopardus*.)

Then a slight variation. '*Culter eius eburneus, id est dens elephanti.*'

And then for the chorus, '*O oculi caeruli! O culter eburneus!*' I sang. '*O oculi caeruli! Ubi est haec puella?*'

In case you don't have Latin club at your school, that all means something like this:

> *A girl with blue eyes, with an ivory knife I seek.*
> *Her knife is a panther, a spotted panther.*
> *Her knife is ivory, the teeth of an elephant.*
> *O blue eyes! O ivory knife!*
> *O blue eyes! Where is this girl?*

A woman with a basket full of onions and a blue cloak over her head tossed a coin to me.

Ping!

At last!

The coin was hardly bigger than my little fingernail and made of the cheapest metal: copper-alloy. But still, it was a coin!

Roman Londoners obviously liked Elizabethan ballads. I sang it out again, clear and bright and with more emotion. I even put my hands together like I was praying and looked up to heaven.

Little copper-alloy coins started pattering down, like the first drops of rain after a dry spell.

Should I stop and pick them up? Or carry on singing?

I didn't want to break the flow, but when the beggar with the withered hand started to edge closer, I lunged to get the coins without stopping the song.

Where to put them?

The flipping Romans had no flipping pockets!

How do you go through life without pockets?

I dropped the little coins down the front of my tunic, hoping they would settle in the place where the cloth pouched over my belt.

It worked.

Thank goodness for my repurposed loincloth. In an age of no pockets, a belt was vital.

Now I had quite a big crowd, and one person even threw a coin the size of my thumbnail that might have been silver.

People were making a strange buzzing hum. But because they were smiling and even laughing I guessed this bee sound was their way of applauding.

Suddenly a skinny woman pushed through the crowd and made straight for me. I recognised the beggar woman from the sores on her skin and recoiled in horror. What if it was leprosy, like in the movie *Ben Hur*? It was contagious even if you barely touched someone.

To my astonishment she swung her fist at me.

I jumped back.

She swung her other fist.

I ran.

Behind me I heard the crowd groan with disappointment. Somebody shouted, *'Mane!'* which I think means 'Wait!'

But I did not wait.

With my coins jingling reassuringly in the pouch at the front of my tunic, I wove between market stalls, careful not to step in rotting veg or donkey droppings.

The stalls gave way to a covered boardwalk on either side of open doorways. The shingle overhang on wooden columns made it look more like a Wild West town than Roman London. Gratefully I left the muddy gravel-studded road and went up onto the boardwalk. As I hurried past the first few doorways on my left, I saw that they opened onto shops.

Behind me I heard shouts of, *'O oculi caeruli!'* and realised a few fans were following me. Maybe the leper woman too. So I ducked into the next shop in the hope of escape.

This store sold lots of objects made out of copper-alloy. It was pretty dim inside, but a couple of hanging oil lamps showed me items like old-fashioned weighing pans like the one held by the statue of justice who stands over a courthouse. A wooden counter also displayed mirrors, chains and oil lamps.

Outside some people ran by shouting, *'O oculi caeruli! O culter eburneus!'*

I shrank back into the darkest corner and saw some bronze-handled knives!

I turned eagerly to the shopkeeper, a short bald man in a leather apron, who was looking at me with narrowed eyes.

'*Excuse me,*' I said in Latin, '*are you Caecilius, seller of knives?*'

The man looked as if I had made a bad smell and tipped his head back for no. '*My name is Naso,*' he said curtly. '*Not Caecilius.*'

I tried one of the other phrases I had memorised. '*Can you tell me where I might buy an ivory knife?*'

Naso's scowl deepened and he pointed to his bronze knives and said something rapid that probably meant, 'Why do you want an ivory one when I have many good knives right here?'

I sighed, then pointed at my feet. '*Sandalia?*' I said, using the Greek word for sandals. Then I plugged it into my memorised phrase. '*Can you tell me where I might buy sandals?*'

At this his scowl relaxed a little and he dipped his head. I was beginning to get that tipping the head back meant no but inclining it forward meant yes, just like in Greece.

He gestured with his left hand and muttered something.

'*Quid?*' I said. 'What?'

'*Sutorius! Sutorius!*' He came out from behind his counter, grabbed a fistful of my tunic and pulled me roughly to the open doorway of his shop. '*Sutorius! Ibi!*' he said. And pointed.

Across the street I saw another row of shops, including one with a wooden shoe instead of a sign above the door, beneath the overhang.

'*Gratias ago*,' I said, and for some reason I put my hands together like my gran when she does namaste after yoga. I even gave a little bow.

I guess that was the right thing to do, because the man gave a gap-toothed smile.

Or maybe he was happy because he had just sent me to be robbed by his pal Sutorius.

25
Bogus Handshake

As I stepped out onto the wooden planks of the walkway I asked myself if I really needed shoes.

Then I saw a rusty nail poking up from one of the uneven planks and muttered to myself, 'Yes, Alex, you need shoes.'

I glanced both ways to make sure the coast was clear, then stepped off the boardwalk and hurried across the gravel road, dancing with every painful step.

Heavy clouds had gathered overhead and it was even darker in the cobbler's shop than it had been in the first shop. I heard tapping down below, and once my eyes adjusted I saw a man sitting on the floor in cobbler's pose, hammering a wooden block between his feet. Behind him ran a low counter with pairs of leather shoes laid out on it. Of each pair, one shoe was right side up to show the top and the other upside down to display various patterns of hobnails on the sole.

'*Salve*,' said the cobbler in a nasal tone and I did a double take. He had a leather nose on a strap around his head. I did *not* want to know what was – or wasn't – underneath.

'*Salve*,' I replied politely. '*Cupio haec*.' I want these.

I pointed to a nice pair of sturdy-looking shoes. They were orange leather with matching leather laces. The hobnail pattern on the base formed an arrow. I reached down the front of my tunic and showed him some of the little coins people had tossed at me.

The cobbler laughed as if I had just told a very funny joke. Then he bent over, reached into a basket on the floor and held up a single leather shoelace. I guessed he was saying that was all my coins could buy.

I fished down my tunic again and found three more tiny coins.

He giggled and held up another shoelace.

Wait! Where was that little silver coin? I was pretty sure silver was worth more than copper-alloy.

I sucked in my stomach and pulled the plaited belt away from my waist.

A tiny *ping!* sounded as the coin struck the brick floor. I bent and managed to nab it before it rolled into the shadows.

I put the coin on the low counter and saw his eyes widen. That meant silver was good. Once again, I pointed at the shoes I wanted.

He lifted his chin for no and pointed to a pair of leather flip-flops.

I also tipped my head back and pointed to a shoe halfway between the flip-flops and the orange shoes. This one was essentially a single piece of leather with a thong that pulled it together over the top of your foot and was then long enough to be tied around your ankles. It had no nails for grip and it would leave part of the top of my foot exposed, but would be better than the flip-flops.

'*Carbatinas cupis?*' said the man, pointing at it. So that type of shoe was called a *carbatina*.

'*Ita,*' I replied. Yes.

The man looked at my bare feet, then reached behind the counter and pulled out a slightly smaller but similar pair and held them up.

'*Bene,*' I replied. Fine.

The noseless cobbler held up a finger as if to say, 'One moment.'

He plucked a brush from a hook on the wall, knelt in front of me and started to brush the mud off my bare feet. It tickled and I couldn't help laughing. The man started laughing too. When my right foot was relatively clean, he put on the shoe and tied it, then looked up at me. I smiled happily and held out my left foot. He brushed it too, and we laughed some more. When he had tied both shoes he stood up and tapped the brush on the door frame to clean it. Then he turned to face me.

'*Tibi placent?*' he said. Do they please you?

I almost nodded, but remembered just in time that a nod could mean no, so I answered in Latin, '*Yes. They please me.*'

The cobbler grinned broadly, revealing no front teeth. Then he held out his hand and said something back to me. I guessed it meant, 'We have a deal.'

Remembering how to do an authentic Roman handshake, I reached for his forearm. But when my hand went past his he looked confused and took a step back.

I smiled and tried again, reaching for just below his elbow. '*Quid agis?*' he cried. That I understood: What are you doing?

'*I'm sorry,*' I told him. I held out my hand and he shook it in the normal way.

So Hollywood had got it wrong.

And so had Martin.

I turned to exit the shop, then turned back. '*Can you tell me where I might find a knife-seller named Caecilius?*'

'*Caecilius?*' he repeated.

'*Yes, Caecilius.*'

He gave this a good few moments of thought, then tipped his head back for no.

'*Bassus ferrarius?*' he suggested. I had no idea what this meant, but I repeated it a few times, thanked him and headed out of the shop in my new shoes.

The *carbatinae* were better than bare feet, but I could still feel the gravel of the road through the thin layer of leather. I suspected I had paid too much for them.

It had started to rain and people with hoods were putting them up.

By doing my humble namaste hands and asking several passers-by and shopkeepers *'Bassus ferrarius?'* I gathered that *ferrarius* meant a blacksmith, and Bassus was the name of one. I finally found him standing on the muddy road outside his shop hammering a piece of red-hot metal. He was a shaggy man in a leather apron, with the worst case of pink-eye I had ever seen.

When he paused in his work I asked him where I could find an ivory-and-iron knife. He shrugged, which I guess meant the same thing then as now. He had never heard of Caecilius either.

So Martin had been wrong about that too. He had given me bad intel.

Really bad.

It was raining harder now and the blacksmith went inside his shop, but I stood where I was, feeling a growing sense of dread.

Martin hadn't warned me that people's Latin was almost unintelligible.

He hadn't told me that the streets were like rivers of mud studded with gravel.

He hadn't told me that Roman Londoners were riddled with disease.

He had described people wearing togas and driving

chariots, but I had not seen one toga or a single chariot.

The information he had given me was wrong too. There was no Caecilius selling bone and iron knives here in Londinium. Or at least not at this time.

Then there was the bogus Roman handshake he had told me about.

The one in all the movies.

And in that moment I realised the truth:

Martin had got all his information from movies.

He hadn't gone back in time at all.

26
Dead Bull

I was still standing outside the blacksmith's workshop. It was now raining heavily, but I was too occupied by my thoughts to care.

If Martin hadn't gone back, how had he lost his foot? And how did he know all that stuff about Mithras? About the masks and the clicking and grunting?

I thought of my advice to Dinu when I first discovered he'd followed me into the past. 'Just stay here. Wait until I get back.'

Then I got it.

That's what Martin had done. He *had* gone back in time. But he had been too scared to venture outside. *He had stayed in the Mithraeum for three days* without ever coming out.

That was how he knew so much about the rites of Mithras but nothing about Londinium in 260 AD.

Then I had another terrible thought.

If Martin had stayed hidden in the Mithraeum on both his trips, then he hadn't interacted with any ancient Roman Londoners. He probably hadn't even been seen by one. Which meant that Solomon Daisy's theory about how we probably can't affect our present world might be wrong.

Maybe we *could* change the future by interacting with people in the past.

Maybe I had already changed the future.

The rain was pelting down, but I was paralysed by dread.

Maybe when I went home my gran wouldn't be living in the third-floor flat of 54 Victoria Gardens. Maybe when I went home I wouldn't even be born. Maybe when I stepped back through the portal I would vanish in a puff of air.

Or maybe when I went home my parents would still be alive and I wouldn't have to live in that tiny flat with my gran but could just visit her from time to time.

All I knew was that I had to abort my mission right away. Some random girl with an ivory knife wasn't worth the risk of an altered future. I had to get home with as little interaction as possible. I had to get back to the time portal in the Mithraeum.

I had been standing in the rain for all this time and I was soaked. By the time I came to my senses, the rain had almost stopped.

Up ahead I saw a grey-haired man in a long tunic and burgundy cloak emerge from the shelter of a shop's awning. I realised with a jolt that he was the first person with grey hair I had seen here. He had a walking stick as tall as himself and was followed by two slaves or maybe bodyguards in pale grey-green tunics.

I hurried through the mud to reach him. *'Excuse me, sir,'* I said, *'where is the Mithraeum?'*

He looked at me suspiciously and said, *'Ain?'* which I knew from my Latin podcast meant, 'Huh?'

'Mithraeum!' I repeated, wiping my rain-drenched face.

He still looked blank so I pulled my knife from my belt and made a downward stabbing motion. *'Taurus mortus!'* I said. Dead bull.

At this he jumped back and brandished his walking stick like a ninja bo-staff. His two slaves cowered behind him. I guessed they weren't bodyguards.

I quickly put my knife back into my belt and held up my hands. Then I tried to think of some other terms associated with Mithras. *'Sol Invictus?'* I said.

'Ah!' He lowered his bo-staff and glanced around. Then he leaned forward and said in a low voice, *'Antrum perseum?'*

I had no idea what *antrum* was, but I knew Mithras wore a Persian cap and that one of the levels was *Persis,* the Persian.

Again I caught myself about to nod, but remembered just in time and said *'Ita!'* Yes!

Bo-Staff pointed and said something else. I understood

the words *pons, dexter, sinister* and *recte* — bridge, right, left and straight on — but not much else.

I thanked him – '*Gratias ago*' – but he was already moving on, tapping his head with his forefinger and saying something to one of his slaves.

I followed at a discrete distance, because he was heading the same way as me.

'*Pons*,' I repeated to myself. And I tried out a phrase under my breath: '*Where is the bridge?*'

In fact we were coming up to a bridge now, but it was only another small one.

The rainstorm had passed and the sun peeped out from between clouds. It made everything look brighter and cleaner. Roman, even. It was almost a shame I had to go back now.

But if there was a risk of my changing the future, then the less interaction I had, the better.

Then I remembered Dinu and stopped in my muddy tracks. Behind me some girls bumped into me and started giggling, but I was too busy thinking about Dinu to take any notice.

If he had drowned, then his body would have floated out to sea, never to be found.

But what if he had managed to crawl ashore? In that case he would surely try to find his way back to the Mithraeum.

Hopefully without interacting with too many people.

I definitely had to get there.

The giggling girls were still behind me and now I felt a

tap on my damp shoulder. I turned to see a girl a little older and a lot taller than me. She had a sapphire blue cloak with a hood. My jaw dropped as I gazed into the most amazing eyes I had ever seen in my life. They were the same colour as her cloak and stood out even more because of the smoky black eyeliner she had painted around them.

I was frozen. Like those people in the Greek myth who looked at Medusa and got turned to stone.

Suddenly she covered her mouth and giggled, and the spell was broken. For the first time I noticed another shorter girl behind her, staring at me wide-eyed.

'*What do you want?*' I said cautiously to the blue-eyed girl.

She said something that sounded like '*Eros?*'

Eros is the Greek god of love, but also a boy's name. She must have mistaken me for someone else. Forgetting about gestures, I shook my head and turned to go, but she grabbed my hand. I was so surprised that I turned back. She said something else that I didn't understand. Her cloak slipped off her head and I saw that she had honey blonde hair in complicated braids pinned to her head.

I put up my hand to show polite refusal.

'*I heard your song,*' she said in Latin. '*What do YOU want from me?*'

I didn't have a clue what she was talking about so I frowned. '*Non comprehendo.*'

That was when she pushed her cloak aside to show me

something dangling from her belt by a short copper chain. It was a folding knife with an ivory handle carved in the shape of a leopard.

I looked back up into those eyes, then back down at the object dangling from her belt.

It was the blue-eyed girl with the ivory leopard knife.

I hadn't found her.

She had found me.

27
Blue Eyes

As I stared open-mouthed at the blue-eyed girl with the ivory knife all the little hairs on my arms lifted up. The spots on the ivory leopard had been picked out in black and the blade was smooth not corroded, but it was definitely the same knife Solomon Daisy had shown me.

I pinched myself hard, and did not wake up.

She was still there, looking down at me with the bluest eyes I had ever seen and smelling oddly like a mixture of church and apple pie. That's when it hit me.

She was real.

A high-pitched time-travel squeal filled my head. My stupid song had worked!

'*Veni*,' she said, and took my hand. I could feel her slender fingers trembling. She pulled me to the side of the road by some stables. The strong scent of mule dung and horse manure could not mask her strange perfume.

She said something to me about Cupid and good omens. But I missed some vital words and stared stupidly.

The blue-eyed girl turned to her friend and said 'I don't think he speaks Latin very well.'

I had understood her! I realised she had spoken in Greek.

'You speak Greek?' I said.

'Yes!' Her blue eyes opened wide. 'Do you?'

Her accent was utterly bizarre, but I understood her.

'Yes,' I said hesitantly. 'I speak Greek. But not well. I am from a faraway land.'

'Oh!' She giggled and covered her mouth with her hand. 'Your accent is so strange!'

'No.' I felt a big smile spread across my face. 'Your accent is strange.'

She giggled again and looked at me with those amazing eyes. The DNA report had stated they were 'blue'. It should have said: *BLUE!*

'What is your name?' I asked, my heart thudding.

'Lollia,' she said. 'My name is Lollia Honorata.'

'Lollia,' I repeated. 'Lollia Honorata.' It was one of the prettiest names I had ever heard. And not just because it was worth four million pounds to me.

She cocked her head. 'What is your name?'

'Alex,' I said, and then quickly corrected myself. 'Alexandros son of Philippos.' I pronounced it the way Gran sometimes did, with the accent on the second syllable.

'Alexandros,' she repeated, in a way that made me shiver.

I managed to tear my gaze away and smiled at Lollia's friend. She had brown hair and was exactly my height, so we were eye to eye. She had also outlined her eyes in smudgy black kohl, but they couldn't compare to Lollia's bewitching blue eyes.

'What is your name?' I asked the girl politely.

Lollia answered for the girl. 'She's just my slave. What does her name matter?'

But the slave-girl spoke anyway. 'Plecta,' she said. Her smile made her look almost pretty. 'My name is Plecta.'

Lollia drew back her arm and slapped the girl's cheek so hard that her hand left a red mark. Then she turned back to me.

'Where are you from?' she said brightly.

My jaw hung open as I looked from Lollia to her slave-girl. Had that really just happened? Had Lollia really just hit the girl? Plecta's head was lowered in submission. I had totally lost my train of thought.

'Excuse me?' I said. 'What did you ask?'

'Where do you come from?'

'Um, a faraway country. My boat sank and I came ashore with only this.' I pointed to my tunic.

'And a knife,' she pointed out.

'I got the knife from a woman who tried to rob me,' I said.

The slave-girl Plecta gasped, but Lollia took no notice.

'*My* knife is magic,' she said, showing me the ivory knife with the leopard handle. 'It keeps away evil and it brought you to me.'

Something made me shiver.

'You're soaking wet,' said Lollia. Without looking at her slave-girl, she snapped her fingers. 'Plecta, give him your palla.'

Plecta immediately took off her brown cloak and held it out to me. I could see bruises on the pale skin of her arms.

'No,' I said, still speaking Greek. 'It's all right. The sun is out now. It will dry me. Please. Let her keep it.'

'As you wish,' said Lollia.

Plecta shot me a grateful look and hesitantly took back her cloak.

Standing at that crossroads in ancient Londinium, I realised that Lollia was just like some of the prettiest girls at my school. Beautiful but mean. I'd have bet some of them would happily slap their friends if they could get away with it.

If Lollia was a Mean Girl, then maybe Plecta was like one of their shy but adoring followers. Or maybe she had no choice. I wondered how she had got the bruises on her arms.

'I told you it would happen this morning,' said Lollia to Plecta. She turned to me to explain, 'All the omens were good. This morning I had an even number of seeds on my roll and the smoke from the altar candle went towards Aphrodite, which almost never happens.'

Although I could understand her almost perfectly, her Greek sounded very strange. Her vowels were round and smooth; they somehow made me think of olives.

'I can't believe I found you,' I said, trying to make my Greek sound more like hers.

She giggled. 'Everyone in the neighbourhood is talking about you!'

Plecta's head came up sharply. 'I was the one who heard about him,' she said, 'when I went to the well for water!'

Lollia ignored her. 'Pater was out – another good omen – so I told the door-slave I was going shopping. But really I came to find you.'

'We really should go back, mistress,' said Plecta. 'You know your father doesn't like you going outside.'

Lollia pinched some skin on her slave-girl's arm and gave it a fierce twist. The girl gasped and once again hung her head in submission. That explained the bruises.

'So why were you seeking me?' Lollia asked brightly.

In the past week I had listened to hours of Latin podcasts. I had memorised a dozen useful sentences and a map of Roman London. I had even learned all about the seven grades of Mithraism.

But I was totally unprepared for this question.

28
Good Omens

'Why was I looking for you?' I repeated, partly to give myself time to think. 'Um, a man who lives in my faraway country sent me to find out if you are well.'

'Your patron? What's his name?'

I couldn't remember the Latin word for Daisy so I made one up. 'Dasius,' I said. Then I remembered that Roman men had at least three names. So I expanded: 'Marcus Solomon Dasius.'

'Does he know my father?' she cried. 'Marcus Lollius Honoratus? He is a dealer in spices and perfume. '

'Um, yes, I think so.'

'Then you are practically in our *familia*. You must come home with me and wait for him.' She caught my hand and gave it a tug. 'We'll get you some dry clothes and better shoes.'

'Do you live near here?'

She pointed. 'Just back there.'

My mind was racing. I probably had enough information about her to get my bonus, but only if the world I knew was still waiting for me. And I realised how much I wanted to get back to that world.

Rule number three: as little interaction as possible.

'I'm sorry,' I said. 'But I lost my slave in the shipwreck. I have to go back across the river and look for him.' I was getting used to speaking Greek with strange round vowels.

Lollia's sapphire eyes got even brighter. 'Oh, Alexandros! Take us with you! We want to see the gladiator games, don't we, Plecta?'

It must have taken a lot of courage for Plecta to do what she did next.

'Mistress,' she said, 'we cannot go there alone. We should not even be out of the house!'

Lollia hauled back to slap Plecta, but I grabbed her wrist. Lollia stared at me in astonishment.

'We don't smack our slaves in my country,' I said gently.

'But she's impudent!'

'No, she cares about you.'

Lollia stamped the muddy road with her foot. 'But it might be my last chance to go! Tertius will never let me see the gladiators.' She looked at Plecta. 'Alexandros can show us the way!'

'I don't know the way!' I protested. Then I frowned at her. 'What do you mean, your "last chance to go"?'

Lollia and Plecta looked at each other. Then Lollia took a deep breath and said, 'In three days I'm getting married.'

I stared. 'Married? Aren't you too young?'

Lollia lifted her chin a little and looked down on me. 'I'll be fourteen in the autumn,' she said. 'And I am a woman, not a child.' Then she grabbed my hands with both of hers. Her fingers had slight calluses on the tips. 'Alexandros! Please come with us? I'm sure the gods have sent you.'

'Isn't it dangerous for you to be out on your own?' I asked. 'Like Plecta said?'

'I won't be on my own. And I have my lucky knife,' she said. 'The leopard of Dionysus will protect me from evil. And all the omens were good this morning.'

My mind was racing.

The blue-eyed girl with the ivory leopard knife had practically fallen into my lap. But I didn't want to mess up my world by interacting too much in this one. On the other hand, if interaction in third-century Roman London *did* have an effect, then it was too late – everything was totally messed up anyway.

And if my world was still there for me, then knowing more about her would guarantee me five million pounds.

Plus, who wouldn't want to see real live gladiators?

I had visited London's Roman amphitheatre once, and I knew it was not too far from the Mithraeum.

Lollia was still clutching my hand. I caught a whiff of her

breath, which was pretty bad. 'Please, Alexandros? Come with us to the amphitheatre at least.'

I took a step back. 'All right,' I said. 'I'll go with you, but you have to tell me all about yourself and especially how you came to be living in Londinium.'

'Oh gay!' she cried. And Plecta whispered, 'Oh gay!' too.

For a minute I wondered what they were on about. Then I realised they were saying, '*Euge!*' which means 'Yay!'

'*Euge!*' I agreed. And smiled at Lollia. 'Lead on!'

29
Leather Bikinis

My gran once told me that when she first moved to London in the 1980s, taxi drivers would refuse to drive her home from the West End because she lived 'South of the River'.

She said other Londoners have always looked down their noses at those of us who live in south London. I guess it was just the same in Roman times, because everyone was heading for the bridge so they could cross over to the northern bank.

As we shuffled along with the other people I tried to get more information about the blue-eyed girl with the ivory knife. 'When did you come to Londinium?' I asked Lollia. 'And where are you from?'

'I was born in Lepcis Magna, in the province of Libya,' she said. 'We came here five years ago, when I was nine. My father was in the army,' she said. 'After he retired, he started working for his uncle as a buyer and seller of spices.'

My stomach gave a ginormous rumble.

Lollia and Plecta shared a look and giggled.

'Are you hungry?' asked Lollia.

Suddenly I *was* hungry. 'Starving!' I said. And then my empty stomach sank as I remembered. 'But I'm fasting.'

'Are you doing a *diatritus*?' asked Lollia.

It was a Greek word, but I had no idea what it meant. 'What's that?'

'A fast lasting three days,' said Lollia. 'You do it to bring on the crisis. I'm an expert on fevers,' she said proudly. 'I get them all the time.'

'I'm doing it for religious reasons,' I lied.

'Oh! Which god do you worship?'

I almost told them I worshipped Jesus Christ, but remembered just in time that Romans liked to throw Christians to the lions.

While I was trying to think of a safe god, Lollia said, 'I worship the Great Mother of course. But Dionysus is my favourite. The leopard is his special pet.'

I frowned. 'Isn't Dionysus all about wine?'

'And music and dance and most of all plays!' said Lollia. 'Pater says Dionysus is the most powerful deity, because he is the god of stories.' She put her hand to her cheek. '*Eheu!*' Alas!

'Is your tooth hurting, mistress?' asked Plecta.

'Yes. The oil of clove has worn off.' Lollia reached down

the front of her tunic and produced a miniature amphora made of bluish-green glass. After using her front teeth to pull out a tiny cork, she tipped some of the golden oil onto her forefinger and rubbed it on one of her lower left molars. When she put back the little cork, I caught a whiff and realised that was the smell I had mistaken for apple pie, probably because my gran puts cloves in her recipe.

We had come to a standstill because we had finally reached the bridge. The road was crowded with braying animals, creaking carts and shouting Londoners. The traffic was hardly moving at all.

'Ask someone what's happened,' Lollia whispered in my ear. 'Just say, "*Quid agitur?*"'

'Why don't you ask someone?' I said.

'Because I'm a girl!'

'I thought you were a woman.'

Lollia rolled her eyes. 'Women can't ask either. It's too bold.'

The man in front of me had a pointy-hooded cloak and a walking stick. I tapped his shoulder. When he turned to look at me I tried not to gasp. He had a big lump of flesh growing out of the side of his cheek and neck. I managed a smile and said politely, '*Quid agitur?*'

He scowled and in heavily accented Latin said something about a donkey. Apparently one had stopped on the bridge and refused to budge.

The man muttered something else. His accent was so strong that I only caught the word *ludi*, which means plays, games or fun.

'Oh no,' said Lollia. 'He says if we're going to the games we'll never make it. They start in an hour.'

Suddenly a great cheer went up and people started laughing and making a bee sound.

'What is it?' I said. 'What's happening?'

'There!' said Lollia, and pointed. 'Acrobat girls!'

Four young women wearing nothing but leather bikinis seemed to be walking on the heads and shoulders of the crowd. Their long dark hair swung in beaded plaits around their shoulders and their bare arms were painted with blue spirals. When one of them did a kind of cartwheel, I realised what was happening.

'I think they're walking on the side of the bridge,' I said. I tried to think of a way to add *like a gymnast on a balance beam* but couldn't think of the words in Greek.

Lollia gasped and looked at Plecta. Her blue eyes sparkled with excitement.

'Mistress, no!' cried Plecta. 'We couldn't!'

'Yes, we could!' said Lollia.

'What?' I asked.

'Plecta used to be an acrobat,' said Lollia. 'She's been teaching me how to do tricks, including walking on the rope.' The word she used was *funambulist*.

I looked at Plecta. 'You mean you could do what those girls just did?'

Plecta inclined her head for yes, her pale cheeks flushed with pleasure.

'No,' I said firmly. 'You two might be able to walk on the side of the bridge. But I can't.'

'Wool fluff!' said Lollia. 'It's easy.'

'We will help you,' said Plecta, and then to Lollia, 'We should do it barefoot, mistress. It will be easier.'

'Yes!' agreed Lollia, and extended her foot so that Plecta could crouch to unlace her pretty red leather shoes. Lollia turned to me. 'I'll lead the way. You can follow me and Plecta will follow you to make sure you don't fall. The trick,' she added, 'is to look at the point where you want to go, the end of the bridge. Oh, and you'd better take off your *carbatinae* too. Tie the laces together and hang them around your neck.'

And so it was that I found myself walking on the right-hand guard rail of Londinium's first bridge.

30
Balance Beam

Walking along the side of London Bridge was terrifying.

First, because it was about twice as long as any of the modern bridges in London, because the Thames was much wider then.

Second, because the oak beam on which we were walking was only about thirty centimetres wide. You might say that is broad enough, but when you have to walk half a kilometre with jeering people on your left and fast-flowing grey water far below you, it is no joke.

Third, because the beam was still wet from the recent downpour.

At first I tried to look at my destination, the end of the bridge, but Lollia was in the way, so instead I kept my eyes fixed on the back of her neck, where the thongs of her red leather sandals were draped.

Plecta had hitched up her dress a little and tied her brown palla around her waist. Lollia had done the same with her sapphire cloak. I could see the pale pink of her tunic and her milky white skin. Whenever I wobbled, I felt Plecta's firm fingertips on the outside of my upper arms, gently keeping me steady.

As I relaxed a little, I began to take in the view.

From here I could clearly see the original 'square mile' of London. Most of the roofs were covered with reddish-orange tiles, but some had pale yellow tiles and a few had both colours together in stripes or zig-zags. One red-roofed building straight ahead rose way higher than the others. I knew from my prep that it was London's basilica. Apparently it was the biggest building north of the Alps.

We were about halfway across the crowded bridge when we saw a stiff little donkey rise above the heads of the people. It was on its back and seemed to float to our side of the bridge before it hung over the Thames. Lollia stopped and I wobbled, but Plecta steadied me from behind. The three of us watched the dead donkey fall into the water below. It was just a little one, and so skinny you could see every rib, but it made a big splash, almost swamping a round coracle. The tide was going out, and for a few moments we watched the skinny carcass float away out to sea, possibly to join poor Dinu.

Down on the bridge, traffic began to move again, but

slowly. We were still making much better time walking on the guard rail.

That was when Lollia started to sing, '*A girl with blue eyes, with an ivory knife in the shape of a leopard I seek,*' to the tune of 'Greensleeves'.

As she sang, she swept her arms gracefully back and forth. I echoed her motions and turned my head to see Plecta doing it too.

After every stanza, Lollia paused and swung out one leg. Plecta and I hesitated and then started doing it in sync with Lollia, at which point the people on the bridge buzzed at us and some even applauded.

For the first time since I had arrived in the past, I was enjoying myself.

'*O cultrum eburneum! O oculi caeruli!*' we sang as we walked.

The sun was shining and a soft breeze was blowing. Now that my tunic was almost dry, I realised the rain had been as good as a shower. I was as clean as when I had first arrived.

I felt good. In fact I felt too good. I kicked out with one foot and nearly lost my balance. But Plecta's firm hands steadied me from behind.

The end of the bridge was almost in sight, my heartbeat was slowing to normal and I felt a strange happy energy. We could do it! We could make it to the north bank and the amphitheatre. Lollia could have her day at the games. Maybe I could watch a few bouts too. Then I would go back to the Mithraeum, where I felt sure Dinu would be waiting patiently. He and I would travel back through the portal to discover the world unchanged. Except that I would have five million pounds in the bank and could look after my gran and would never have to worry again.

I kept my gaze fixed on Lollia's back, with her graceful arms extended and the blonde plaits intertwined on her head and the thongs of her red leather sandals draped around her milky-white neck.

We had almost reached the other end of the bridge when something terrible happened.

I fell.

But not in the way you think.

31
Lucky Dionysus

There was something about the back of Lollia's neck that made me go all squiggly inside.

I felt an urge to kiss it.

You've probably guessed what happened.

On that bridge, looking at Lollia's slender neck, I fell in love with the blue-eyed girl from Africa.

NO! I mentally shouted at myself. *This cannot be happening. This is the worst idea ever. Lollia is a Mean Girl who is going to DIE and there's nothing I can do to save her.*

Once again I felt dizzy.

Once again Plecta's hands steadied me and restored my balance.

There were soldiers up ahead, where the bridge ended. One of them was giving us a look so intense I could almost feel it. I understood why ancient Greeks and Romans believed that eyes sent out tiny particles that could harm a person.

I hissed to Plecta, 'I don't think we're supposed to be up here. We'd better get down or the soldiers will be angry.'

Plecta leaped down lightly and held up her hands to her mistress. I didn't want to seem wimpy in front of Lollia so I jumped without help, but I landed awkwardly, almost twisting my ankle.

'Are you all right?' asked Plecta, her brown eyes full of concern.

'Yes,' I muttered. I bent to put on my new leather shoes so she wouldn't see my eyes watering.

Plecta knelt to do the laces of Lollia's pretty leather shoes and then put on her own shoes, which were cheap *carbatinae* like mine.

By the time we reached the soldiers, they were going through the leather satchel of a trinket merchant and let us pass without a glance.

I heaved a sigh of relief.

The three of us were swept along by the crowd and I felt a thrill as Lollia grabbed my hand. She was holding Plecta's hand too, so that I was on her right and Plecta on her left.

'I think the amphitheatre is that way,' said Lollia, pointing north-west with her chin.

'That seems right,' I agreed. 'That's the way most people are heading.'

Now the buildings around us looked Roman. Some had columns in front. A few were made of stone not brick. One building resembled a small version of the British Museum, with a flat triangle above pillars. At the foot of the steps leading up to it was a big block of marble with the charred remains of some animal on top. It looked like a failed attempt at a barbecue.

'What happened there?' I pointed.

'That's the Temple of Jupiter,' said Lollia. 'Today is one of his special days. That's why the gladiators are doing their games.'

'What's that big block with the dead animal on top?'

Lollia gave me a funny look. 'That's the altar of course. They probably sacrificed that sheep at dawn. They usually distribute some of the cooked meat, but I think we're too late.'

'Do you actually believe in Jupiter?' I asked Lollia.

'Of course,' she said. 'And in the Great Mother. But I told you: Dionysus is my special protector.' She let go of my hand to touch the knife at her belt.

'Did you buy the leopard knife here in Londinium?' I asked her.

'No, it's from the place I used to live, Lepcis Magna,' she said.

I shivered as I remembered that one of the studies on her bones indicated that she might have grown up in north Africa. 'Is Lepcis Magna in Africa?' I asked her.

'Yes, in a province called Libya.'

'Tell me about it?'

'I can't tell you much. Just that it was hotter than here and the buildings were much bigger and made of marble. I remember a huge arch as tall as three houses. And some scary Medusa faces on a big building. But my sisters and I hardly went into our own courtyard, much less the town. Mother said the sun would turn our fair skin brown and nobody would want to marry us. That's why she kept us indoors so much.'

'So you never went out?'

'Hardly ever. Just for some festivals and processions.'

'What did you do all day?'

'The same thing I do here in Londinium. I weave cloth.'

'Don't you go to school?'

'Girls don't go to school. My father taught me enough letters to get by. My mother taught me to weave. And some other special skills,' she added mysteriously.

I imagined Lollia as a toddler sitting at a little loom, and my heart melted for her.

'Why did you leave Lepcis Magna?' I asked.

Lollia looked at me wide-eyed. 'Because of the plague,' she whispered. 'The great plague of Carthage.'

32
Zombie Apocalypse

'Plague?' I cried, my voice louder than intended. 'Like a contagious plague?'

People around me shrank back and Lollia hissed, 'Shhh!' She and Plecta both made the sign against evil by poking their right thumb between the first two fingers of their right fist. 'Of course the plague was contagious,' she whispered. 'Don't you have plagues where you come from?' Her breath in my ear made me shiver.

'No,' I murmured. 'What happened?'

'It was horrible. People had blood coming from their noses and ears and even their eyes.'

I stared at her in shock. She must have taken my shock for interest because she told me more.

'The sick people were so thirsty that they could never drink enough.' Her voice was still low. 'It was as if all the water in the world could not satisfy them. The wells and fountains were full of dead bodies. Then there were pits full of corpses. The priests sprinkled white powder on them and burned them.'

'It sounds like the zombie apocalypse,' I muttered to myself in English. But of course the word *apocalypse* is Greek, and she looked up sharply.

'Yes,' she said. 'It was like the apocalypse. First my mother died, then my two sisters. Then grandparents, uncles, aunts. It seemed like the end of the world. But somehow my father and I survived.'

We had reached the amphitheatre and were in a queue of people shuffling towards the entrance.

'How?' I said. 'How did you survive and not the others?'

'My lucky knife,' she said. 'Pater gave it to me for my ninth birthday, three days before the plague struck. I didn't realise until later. Now I will never take it off.'

'Why did you come to Londinium?' I asked.

'Because it's as far as we could get from Lepcis Magna, where all those terrible things happened.'

'Was the voyage hard?' I asked.

'You must know the answer,' she said. 'But yes. It was cold and wet. Even the ship was crying.'

'The ship cried?'

'Yes. She was always groaning and squeaking. We had to sleep in a shack called a cabin, like a wooden hut on deck.'

'Tell him about the sea-monster,' said Plecta.

Lollia said, 'Once we saw a sea-monster. The sailors called it Leviathan.'

'Were you with them?' I asked Plecta. 'I thought everybody in Lepcis Magna died.'

Lollia put her arm around Plecta. 'We stopped at many ports along the way, and Pater bought Plecta at the slave market of Massilia. I had come down with a fever and he wanted a girl or woman to nurse me.'

'How long were you on the ship?' I asked.

'Almost three months.'

I couldn't imagine that. I think the longest journey I have ever taken is ten hours.

'Look, mistress!' cried Plecta. 'We are here!'

Sure enough we were going through an arch into Londinium's fine stone amphitheatre.

I was about to see real Roman gladiator games.

33
White Teeth

If I tell you which football team I support, will you promise not to hate me?

I'll give you a clue. It's not Arsenal, Spurs or Chelsea.

It's Fulham.

My dad supported Fulham. About a month before he and Mum died in that car crash he took me to a match. So you can't blame me for supporting them. It was practically my dad's dying wish.

Going to Londinium's amphitheatre was a bit like attending a match at Fulham.

Apart from a few families, the crowd was mainly men.

But instead of thermos flasks, the punters clutched leather wine-skins.

And instead of coolers, they had shoulder bags in woven wool or leather. (I could see something like a baguette sticking out of one.)

Some people even brought their own cushions, like today. The one thing they didn't need was a ticket. Entry was free as long as there were still seats. And we were among the last to get them. We managed to find three together, though they were quite high up and the sun was in our eyes. I heard something like organ music, though I couldn't tell where it was coming from. And I kept catching whiffs of incense.

Then I noticed that the people in nearby seats were staring at me. Did something about me betray the fact I came from the future?

'Why is everyone staring at me?' I asked Lollia.

She and Plecta exchanged a glance and then started giggling. Let me tell you: girls giggling is the same in the third century AD as it is today.

'Don't you know?' said Lollia. She looked at Plecta and they both covered their mouths.

My pride was stung. 'It is because I look strange?'

'Not at all!' said Lollia. 'It's because you're beautiful!'

'I'm *beautiful*?' I stared at her, and the two girls both gave the single downward nod for yes.

'Your skin,' said Lollia. 'It is so smooth and clear.' She reached out and stroked my cheek with the back of her forefinger.

It made me shiver, but in a good way.

'Also your hair is so shiny.' She ran her fingers through

my hair, which was still slightly damp from the rain shower that had washed me clean.

'Your eyes are very bright,' added Plecta shyly.

'And your teeth,' said Lollia. 'Show us your teeth!'

Feeling a bit self-conscious, I opened my mouth so they could look inside. That's when I had a flash of déjà vu that took me back to my headteacher's office at the start of this adventure.

'Oh!' they cried, and Lollia's eyes actually filled with tears. 'They are perfect!' she said, and clasped her hands over her heart. 'How I wish I had teeth like yours.'

'How do you make them so perfect?' asked Plecta shyly.

I considered saying, 'My grandmother makes me brush

twice a day and floss before bed.' Instead I shrugged. 'Just lucky, I guess.'

Plecta whispered into Lollia's ear, but not so quietly that I couldn't hear. 'Alexandros is like Eros, the god of love.'

'Yes!' breathed Lollia, and clapped her hands.

I sat up straighter and tried not to look smug. I wondered what the kids in my class would say if they knew I was a love god in Roman London.

Then I had a thought. 'Wait!' I said. 'Isn't Eros the same as Cupid? That naked baby with the wings and arrows?'

'Look!' Without answering my question, Lollia gripped my arm and pointed to the arena. 'I think the show is about to start.'

Down on the yellowish-grey sand of the arena, a man in a cream tunic with two vertical red stripes had come out. Behind him was a man in a short red tunic with a strange-looking trumpet. He brought the horn to his lips and blew a fanfare of five or six rising notes. The murmuring audience fell silent but a moment later erupted into cheers as some men started to come out onto the sand.

They were gladiators! Real. Live. Gladiators.

At first I was excited. But pretty soon after that I felt disappointed.

They weren't muscular and buff. Most of them were stocky, even fat.

None of them looked like Russell Crowe in the classic

film *Gladiator*. In fact, one of them reminded me of Bob from Croydon who had fixed our boiler the previous winter. He held his helmet under one arm.

'*Those* are the gladiators?' I said to Lollia.

'I don't know,' she said, without taking her eyes off the men. 'I've never seen one before.'

I turned around and saw a fluffy-bearded teenager in a cream-coloured blanket behind us. '*Excuse me*,' I said in Latin, '*are those the gladiators?*'

He gave a curt downward nod for yes. '*Ita vero.*'

Then the whole arena gasped and I turned back to see a blond boy wearing what looked like a baby's nappy and padded shin-guards. He held a tall trident in one hand and a net in the other and he looked familiar.

When I was in Year Five I did a project on different types of gladiators. This one looked like a *retiarius*, the net man, except he didn't have a shoulder guard.

Lollia said, 'Look at that one. He's beautiful.'

'I think he's called a *retiarius*,' I said. 'They fight with net and trident.'

'Find out his name,' commanded Lollia. 'Ask that youth behind us.'

I turned back to the fluffy-bearded teenager sitting behind us. I realised his blanket was a toga. It was the first toga I had seen up close. '*Excuse me*,' I said in Latin again, '*do you know his name?*'

'The *retiarius*?' said Fluffy Beard. 'His name is Dionysus but they are calling him Dinu.'

Already the crowd was chanting, *'Dinu! Dinu! Dinu!'*

Dinu?

My head whipped around and I squinted down at the *retiarius* with the floppy blond hair.

No wonder he looked familiar.

Dionysus the *retiarius* was Dinu Balan, my arch-flipping-nemesis.

34
Parental Advisory

Dinu Balan wasn't a body floating in the Thames. He was a gladiator fighting in London's arena.

I literally pinched myself to make sure I wasn't dreaming. How could Dinu have become a gladiator in less than twenty-four hours? It was impossible.

Or was it?

Maybe someone had fished him out of the river and, like me, he had tried to think of a way to earn money for clothes and shoes. His obvious big strengths were that he was – well, big and strong.

So here he was, armed with a fishing net and a giant fork.

'*Furcifer!*' I muttered between clenched teeth.

'He's called Dionysus!' breathed Lollia. 'Just like the god I worship.' She gripped Plecta's hands. 'Isn't he beautiful?'

Without taking her eyes from him, Plecta gave the single downward nod for yes.

A minute ago they'd called me beautiful. Now they were gazing at him as if he were a god.

'Double *furcifer!*' I muttered. I had to regain control of this situation. Fast. I couldn't have them crushing on Dinu.

'I know him!' I said. 'I know that *retiarius*.'

Both girls looked at me.

'You know him?' squeaked Lollia.

'Better than that,' I said. 'I own him. He's my slave. Remember? I lost him when we were washed ashore.'

Lollia's eyes grew wide. 'That beautiful boy is your slave?'

I ground my teeth.

'Where are they going?' asked Plecta, as the gladiators all marched out again.

The man with the striped tunic came into the centre of the arena and held up both hands.

'*Today, if great Jupiter is favourable,*' he said in clear slow Latin, '*we will execute criminals, pit beasts against each other and celebrate his festival with combat of gladiators.*'

Everyone buzzed and some did a kind of applause with cupped hands that Lollia called 'roof-tiles'.

'But first,' he said, 'the sacrifice of a goat.'

A man with a toga draped over his head came out. He was followed by a goat with a fat red ribbon around its middle. Then came four young men wearing linen kilts and nothing else. One held a flat silver bowl, one a knife, one a jug and the fourth one trilled on a wooden flute.

The flute-player stopped long enough for the priest to ask the goat if it submitted to sacrifice. He sprinkled water from the jug onto its head and it gave the downward nod yes.

The flutes started up again and then, quick as lightning, the young man with the knife cut the goat's throat and the other youth caught the blood in his bowl. The crowd cheered. Although we were high up, I had to look away.

The girls acted as if they had seen this sort of thing every day of their lives; they were busy whispering about a woman with a tasselled parasol and two dark-skinned bodyguards sitting three rows down.

The beast fight that came next made the sacrifice of the goat seem like an old ladies' tea party.

It was awful. They made a skinny bull fight a scruffy bear. The two animals were so old and tired that neither of them could kill the other. In the end the referee awarded the victory to the bear and put something like a Christmas wreath on his head. Two men in masks came out and cut the bull's throat. It was horrible but the people loved it. They cheered when the bull finally stopped twitching. Musicians led the staggering bear out of the arena.

Then came an announcement about criminals, and some men were paraded with forked branches on their necks and their hands bound to the straight part of the branch behind them. It looked really uncomfortable and I guessed it was the ancient version of handcuffs.

'Who are they?' I asked Lollia.

'*Furciferi*,' she said, using the Latin word. Crooks. And at last I understood what the word meant: someone who deserves to wear a crooked branch.

'What will they do with them?' I asked in Greek.

'I don't know.'

'They'll torture them,' said the fluffy-bearded teenager behind us. I should have guessed he was educated enough to know Greek.

I made a mental note to keep my voice down.

Then I immediately forgot the mental note as some men with hot pokers began to torture the handcuffed men.

I'm not even going to hint at what they did. It's too awful. Lollia and Plecta screamed and covered their eyes, but tons of people around us were laughing and cheering. Presently Lollia, who had been peeking through her fingers, took her hands from her face and watched.

'Do you like this?' I whispered in her ear.

'It's horrible but also exciting,' she said, her eyes fixed on the arena.

Plecta still had her palla over her face and now her fingers were in her ears to drown out the screams. I didn't need to ask what she thought.

At last it was over and the master of ceremonies – or whatever he was called – announced that it was finally time for the gladiatorial combats.

Everyone buzzed and some people did the 'roof-tile' clapping.

To my astonishment, Dinu was the first gladiator to come out onto the sand. When he was joined by Bob the Boiler-Man, I guessed they were like the support band at a rock concert, warming up the crowd for the main event.

I felt a tap on my shoulder and turned to see Fluffy Beard. He leaned forward and said in Greek, 'Did I hear you say you own him?'

'Yes,' I said. 'He's my property.'

'Then you should redeem him.'

'Oh yes!' cried Lollia, clutching my left arm. 'You must redeem him!'

'I don't know how,' I said.

'I do,' said Fluffy Beard, and stretched out his hand. 'I am Aelius Claudius Epapras,' he added. 'Lawyer.'

I shook his hand and said, 'Excuse me, but you don't look old enough to be a lawyer.'

Epapras sat up straight and said with great dignity, 'I am almost eighteen and I have already won four cases.'

'*Please* help us redeem him?' pleaded Lollia.

'If he survives!' gasped Plecta. 'Look!'

We all turned back to the arena. Bob the Boiler-Man had put on his helmet and was facing off with Dinu.

In my school project about gladiators, I had written that the *retiarius* is always paired with a *secutor*. I was pleased to see

I had got it right. Bob was wearing a smooth bullet-shaped helmet with tiny round eyeholes. He had a big shield and a wide belt above his nappy. And he brandished a double-edged *gladius*, the short but deadly sword from which gladiators get their name.

Dinu on the other hand was dressed in nothing but his big nappy and leg padding. His net looked like a lady's shawl and his long, thin trident looked about as strong as a toothpick.

'Oh no!' cried Lollia, gripping my hand so hard it hurt. 'Dinu is doomed.'

35
Bob the Boiler-Man

Dinu the Retiarius and Bob the Boiler-Man were terrible gladiators.

For a long time they just circled each other. The crowd jeered. It was starting to get ugly, with a few people throwing rotten cabbages, when Dinu tripped on his own net and almost fell. At this, Bob the Boiler-Man lunged. But Dinu managed to stay upright by swinging out with his trident, which just clipped Bob's helmet.

The crowd cheered as Bob staggered back. I'm guessing the blow to his helmet was making his head ring like a bell.

Then Dinu gave a half-hearted jab in Bob's direction, and by some miracle he actually made contact with Bob's thigh. Worse, he made Bob bleed. It didn't look too bad from twelve rows up, but I'm guessing it really stung. Now Bob was swinging wildly with his sword and I realised that Dinu's blow to his helmet had turned it slightly and Bob couldn't see! Then Dinu got tangled in his net again and this time he fell down.

The crowd loved it. They were jeering and laughing and calling out and some of them were making the bee sound.

As I watched Dinu desperately try to get free of the net while Bob swung blindly in the wrong direction, I felt a strange mix of emotions.

On the one hand, I wanted Dinu to beat the guy to a pulp, because Dinu was from Wandsworth Academy and also from my century.

But I couldn't help thinking how convenient it would be if Dinu was out of the picture. Especially as Lollia was now completely ignoring me and gazing at him with wide-eyed panic.

I came to my senses.

How could I even think such a terrible thought?

Guilt made me yell, 'Come on, Dinu!' in English, without thinking about it.

Somehow he heard me and looked up.

When he saw me his expression changed from despair to delight. He freed his foot, jumped up and shouted, 'Wimpy!'

Bob must have heard Dinu's voice, because he whirled around and started slashing in a much more dangerous way.

'Watch out, Dinu!' I bellowed. 'Use the net to get his sword!'

Dinu nodded, swung the net and missed.

Bob's sword took the top off his trident, making it a no-dent.

The crowd gasped. Plecta screamed. Lollia squeezed my hand.

Dinu flung away the useless trident and swung his net again. This time he missed the sword but somehow managed to flick the net around Bob's ankles. Dinu gave a tug and his opponent came crashing down. Right on his sword!

'Argh!' I gasped. 'Own goal!'

Poor Bob screamed, twitched and then lay still. A pool of blood started to spread out on the sand beneath him.

Plecta screamed again and covered her eyes, but Lollia did something that astonished me.

She cheered.

And when the referee guy placed a wreath on Dinu's head she stood up, cupped her hands to her mouth and cried in Greek, 'We love you, Dinu!'

36
Fluff Beard

'Quickly,' said Epapras in Greek. 'We've got to go now, before some rich matron tries to buy him. He's going to be very popular. Follow me.'

He stood up and started along his row.

'Come on, Alexandros!' Lollia stood up. 'We've got to redeem your slave.'

'Do I?' I muttered. But of course I did, so I sighed deeply and followed them along the row of grumpy spectators whose view we were blocking. Once onto the central aisle, Epapras led us higher instead of lower. At first I wondered what he was doing. But when we got to the top I saw an arched doorway and dim stairs going down.

This was the exit.

It was also the toilets, if the stench was anything to go by.

No wonder Lollia's dad had forbidden her to go to the games. It wasn't exactly the family funfair in Battersea Park.

I tried to breathe through my mouth, but it didn't help much. Once I almost slipped in a puddle. My stupid Roman shoes had no grip – their sole was just leather.

I noticed Epapras was holding up the hem of his toga so it didn't drag, and that it was starting to sag at the back, showing two vertical red stripes on his tunic.

At last we reached the bottom and were out into the grey afternoon.

'This way,' said Epapras, and led us around the curve of the big amphitheatre. 'My father bought a bodyguard here last year,' he explained. 'That's how I know where to go.'

He stopped at an arched doorway where two soldiers stood guard. They weren't keen to let us through. 'No entry!' snapped one. 'Performers and organisers only.'

'My name is Aelius Claudius Epapras,' said Epapras in Greek, 'son of Aelius Claudius Nicon of Pergamum. My client has business with the lanista. I can either summon him to court or have a brief word now. I only need a few moments of his time,' he added.

The guard rolled his eyes. 'All right,' he sighed, and stood aside.

A short time later we found ourselves at the entrance of a big dim space beneath the amphitheatre. It was the gladiators' changing area, and it smelled of sawdust and sweat, with just a tang of blood.

The lanista stood with his arms folded across his chest,

blocking our entry. He was a big man with curly grey hair, a squashed nose and hard brown eyes. He looked like a mafia boss from TV and I got a chill just looking at him. Lollia stood on tiptoes, trying to peep over his shoulder into the room full of gladiators preparing for their next bout.

I saw Dinu a moment before she did. He was sitting on a bench against a wall looking dejected, even though he had the victor's garland on his head. He was still wearing the pale blue tunic from the Mithraeum and his bare feet were chained at the ankles.

'There he is!' cried Lollia. 'Dinu!'

Dinu looked up, and when he saw me his face broke into a huge smile. 'Wimpy!' He jumped up from the bench. 'You found me!'

'That is my client's slave,' said Epapras to the lanista. 'We demand that you return him immediately.'

'What proof do you have?' said the lanista. 'Where are his papers?'

They were speaking in Greek so I chipped in, using my best rounded-vowel ancient Greek accent.

'He is my slave,' I said, 'and I can prove it. We both come from a faraway land. Only he and I know the language. I can give him commands known only to me.'

The lanista raised an eyebrow. 'Very well.' He stood to one side.

As the four of us entered, most of the gladiators stared

at us. I suppose we did look strange: a kid who looked like Eros, with a fluff-bearded lawyer and two girls.

I stared back. An uglier bunch of men I have never seen in my life. Over near the entrance to the arena, where it was brightest, a man in a leather apron was sewing up a wounded gladiator. The doctor stopped mid-stitch and his patient hoicked himself up on his elbows, which must have hurt like crazy. It was Bob the Boiler-Man – he was alive!

I turned to Dinu, who was now flanked by two of the biggest and ugliest gladiators. 'If you want me to get you out of this,' I said in English, 'then do as I say. Remember, you're my slave.'

'Dinu!' cried Lollia in Greek. 'I love you!'

'What did she say?' asked Dinu. 'She is beautiful.'

'Nothing,' I said. 'She said nothing. Now focus!'

He grinned. 'All right, Wimpy.'

'And don't call me Wimpy! Address me as either *Kyrie* or *Domine*.'

'*Yes, master*,' he said, using the Latin.

I turned to the lanista. 'Watch,' I said. 'I will tell him to dance.'

I turned to Dinu and said in English, 'Dance!'

Dinu thought for a moment, then did 'The Carlton' which – like I said – was popular at our school. He had a big cheesy smile on his face as he double-snapped the air to the right of his shoulder and then to the left. The chain around his left ankle jingled when he tried to kick his legs out.

Instead of making the sign against evil, all the gladiators laughed. Even Bob the Boiler-Man, who then winced in agony. Behind me I heard the girls giggle. I guess I had been doing it wrong back in the marketplace.

'Next I'm going to tell him to pretend to be dead,' I told the lanista (and anybody else who could understand Greek). To Dinu I said, 'Play dead!'

With a shy glance at Lollia, Dinu got down on the sawdust-strewn floor, lay on his back with his hands folded across his chest and closed his eyes.

The gladiators applauded. Two came panting from their bout in the arena and looked around for praise, but everyone was watching Dinu. The two gladiators who were supposed to be up next also lingered by the exit.

Dinu was up on his feet again. He was looking at Lollia with a goofy grin on his face. She was gazing back with open adoration.

This had to be stopped.

I had a clever plan. I turned to the lanista. 'Next,' I said, 'I'm going to ask him to act like a dog.'

A few of the gladiators laughed, and the two who were due to fight had to be shoved out into the arena.

'What are they laughing about?' said Dinu.

'I want you to act like a dog.'

Dinu looked from me to Lollia and then back at me again.

'No,' he said. 'It will make me look stupid.'

I took a deep breath. 'Dinu,' I said, 'if you want to get out of here alive you have to do this. Act like a dog!'

Reluctantly, he got down on his hands and knees and growled.

The gladiators roared with laughter, but the girls looked shocked. Dinu's face went pink.

I told them what my next command would be.

At this even the lanista grinned and all the gladiators clapped as those who understood translated for the others.

'Alex, no!' whispered Plecta. 'That's cruel!'

'Why do they laugh?' said Dinu, still on his hands and knees. 'What will you make me do next?'

I tried hard not to smile. 'One last thing and then we're free,' I said. 'You've got to bark like a dog.'

Dinu stood up and brushed the sawdust from his hands. 'Absolutely not,' he said. 'They may kill me if they wish, but I will not bark like dog.'

37
Barking Mad

Of course I didn't make Dinu bark. Like Plecta said, that would have been really cruel. Plus, Lollia put her hands together and gave me a pleading look.

So I relented and got him to pat his head and rub his stomach at the same time.

'Now that my client has proved his claim on the slave,' said Epapras to the lanista, 'please release him into our hands.'

The lanista shrugged. 'Of course,' he said. 'You may take him as soon as you have reimbursed me.'

It was a word I didn't understand. 'What does he want?' I asked Fluff Beard.

'He says he paid for him,' said Epapras. And to the lanista, 'How much did you pay for him?'

'Two hundred sesterces,' said the lanista.

'I don't believe you,' said Epapras. 'Nobody in their right mind would pay that much for a slave with no papers.'

'I've got a hundred sesterces!' Lollia held up a small gold coin.

'No, mistress!' cried Plecta. 'That's part of your dowry!'

Lollia drew back her left hand to slap her, but I caught her wrist.

'I told you,' I said. 'I don't believe in striking slaves.'

'And that's why your own slave doesn't obey you,' said the lanista. He took the coin from Lollia, pulled a key from a chain on his belt and bent to unlock Dinu's shackles. 'Take him and go! Before I change my mind.'

'Thank you,' said Epapras. But Lollia had already grabbed Dinu's hand and was pulling him out of the gladiators' changing room.

The rest of us followed.

As soon as we were back outside the amphitheatre, Dinu turned to me. 'How did you find me?'

'Dumb luck,' I said. 'The same way I found Lollia,' I pointed to Lollia, who was looking back and forth at us.

'What do you mean?' said Dinu.

'She's the blue-eyed girl with the ivory leopard knife,' I said. 'The one the big bazillionaire is paying me five million pounds to find.'

Dinu's jaw dropped. 'She is worth five million?'

'Not her personally – just the information I get out of her.'

Someone tugged at my tunic. It was Fluffy Beard. He was pointing at a fat middle-aged man making his way straight towards us. 'Do you know that man?' he asked.

The fat man wore a brown-and-red-striped tunic and an embroidered skullcap on his bald head.

'Great Mother protect me!' choked Lollia. 'It's Tertius.'

'Who?' I said.

'The man I'm supposed to marry. Somehow he's found me. Dinu! Come!'

To my astonishment, she grabbed Dinu's hand and tugged. But he stood solid as a rock, not understanding what was happening.

'*Veni!*' she said in Latin, tugging harder. Either he understood, or he finally got the message. He nodded, and when Lollia pulled up the hem of her tunic and started to run, he and Plecta followed.

I looked back at Lollia's middle-aged fiancé, who had also broken into a trot.

I looked at Epapras, who was frowning. 'Don't run,' he said. 'It will make you look guilty.'

I looked back towards Dinu and the girls. I was just in time to see them swerving into an alley between timber-and-plaster buildings. If I left it any longer, I would never find them again.

'Triple *furcifer!*' I cursed. Then, with an apologetic shrug to Epapras, I raced after them.

38
Cleopatra Eyes

I had been running up and down alleys for about five minutes when an arm shot out and I was tugged into a kind of dim porch before a blue painted door.

'Got you!' said Dinu.

'Oh thank God,' I gasped, resting my hands on my knees and trying to catch my breath. 'I haven't run so much since last sports day.'

'Is he coming?' asked Dinu, peeping into the alley.

'No!' I was still gulping air and trying not to pass out. 'I think I lost him. And I thought I'd lost you too! I don't know what –'

The words died on my lips as I raised my head to look at him. He was wearing Lollia's tunic, and her sapphire palla was draped around his shoulders. Plecta had been using something like my gran's kohl crayon to make his eyes look like Cleopatra's.

'Flippin' heck!' I said. 'Why are you dressed like that?'

He grinned and shrugged. 'So they don't find us.'

I turned to look at Lollia. In the dim light of this dark doorway in a narrow alley, I could see she had put on his pale blue tunic and was undoing all the little plaits in her hair. Already half of it fell down in crinkly waves.

'Look!' said Dinu as he pulled the palla over his head. 'Do I look like girl?'

My jaw dropped. 'Yeah,' I said. 'You kind of do.'

'Pretty girl?'

In fact the black around his blue eyes made him look surprisingly pretty. But I wasn't going to give him the satisfaction of hearing that, so I turned to Lollia. 'What's happening?' I asked her in Greek.

She gave me a radiant smile. Her pale cheeks were pink. 'You and Dinu are going to dress up as rich girls, and we're going to pretend to be your slaves.'

'Why?' I said.

'So we can hide in here,' she said, pointing. 'It's a women's bath-house.'

'Wait . . . What?'

'Hold still,' said Plecta, and brought the kohl crayon close to my eyes. 'This will only take a moment.' I noticed her cheeks were flushed too.

'Alexandros,' said Lollia, who was still undoing her plaits, 'take off your tunic and trade with Plecta.'

'No way!' I protested. 'I've got nothing on underneath. Why can't I wear this? it's almost the same as Plecta's, just a different colour.'

'No. Girls' tunics are longer.'

'Look!' I said, undoing my belt. 'Without the belt it's long.'

'It has to reach the ground,' said Lollia. 'You must trade.'

'I have an under-tunic,' said Plecta. 'As soon as you take off yours, I will give you mine.'

Reluctantly I put my belt and knife on the ground, then turned to face the corner of the porch.

'Hurry!' commanded Lollia. 'If someone opens the door and sees us then we'll be exposed.'

'I can't be more exposed than I am now,' I muttered, quickly pulling off my tunic.

'Here,' came Plecta's voice, and she handed me her longer tunic. I was half hoping it would be too small, but it fit me perfectly and even touched the ground.

She also gave me her belt, which was woven of brown, cream and red wool in a twisty pattern, and I gave her my plaited rag one. I kept my knife, however, sticking it in my new belt.

I turned to see Lollia undoing her last plait. With her golden hair falling in waves around her shoulders she looked lovelier than ever.

She adjusted Plecta's palla over my head and showed me how to drape it by putting one end back over my shoulder.

I let the other side hang down to hide the knife in my belt.

Suitably arrayed, I took a deep breath and knocked on the bath-house door.

Presently a thin woman in a pale green tunic answered. *'How much?'* I asked her in Latin. I tried to make my accent sound like Lollia's.

'Two dupondii,' she replied, holding up two fingers.

I gestured to Plecta, who produced the right coins from a pouch around her neck. A mosaic on the floor reminded me to step over the threshold with my right foot first.

A dim corridor brought us into a changing room with oversized wooden pigeonholes on the wall for clothes. Two muscular ladies in pale green tunics and matching headscarves glared at us. Dinu had the sense not to stare back. Luckily he hadn't started to shave and had nice smooth cheeks.

Needless to say, my cheeks were smooth as a baby's bottom too.

Obviously we couldn't follow the usual procedure of leaving our clothes in a locker. While I was wondering what on earth to do, Lollia turned to the bath-house bouncers. 'My mistress has an urgent message for her friend,' she said briskly. 'We won't be long.'

'Tertius will never find us in here,' she whispered in Greek as we moved out of the changing room.

The next room was dimmer and warmer, with small high

windows and a wooden bench running around the wall. There was a pile of tea towels on a table in the centre. As I followed the girls, I glimpsed some women sitting on the benches wearing nothing but the little tea towels.

Dinu turned his head to have a better look, but I gave his blue shawl a tug and hissed 'Don't stare!'

The third room was the dimmest so far. Steamy too. Just as well, as out of the corner of my eye I could see a pair of totally naked women. But I kept my eyes firmly on the back of Lollia's neck.

'Ow!' muttered barefoot Dinu. 'Hot, hot, hot!'

Even through the leather of my shoes I could feel the heat of the bricks. There must be one of those hypo-thingies underneath. You know – the ancient Roman version of underfloor heating.

'Wait for us here,' said Lollia, pushing us down onto a bench. 'We need the latrine.'

I translated for Dinu.

He grinned. 'Here is good,' he said, as Lollia and Plecta left the steam-room.

I glanced at Dinu and he glanced back at me. It was the first time we had been alone since we had been swept out into the Thames.

39
Steam Heat

'Thank you for saving me,' said Dinu after a moment. 'You are good friend.'

I snorted. 'I'm not your friend, Dinu.'

'Maybe not. But at least you always bring me crisps.'

I stared at him in astonishment and then had to look away. Lollia's sapphire palla made his Cleopatra eyes look almost as blue and beautiful as hers. It was unnerving.

'You're not my friend,' I said through gritted teeth. 'You're a bully. You steal my crisps.'

From the corner of my eye I saw him cock his head. 'No. You bring them for me because you are nice.'

'Are you crazy? I bring them for me. I only give them to you because you'll beat me up if I don't.'

'Beat you up? Have I ever beat you up?'

I thought about this. 'No. But you stand about a foot taller than me and twice my weight, and say, "Give me your crisps."'

Dinu nodded happily. 'And you give because you know my mother cannot afford breakfast.' He patted my back. 'You are a good friend.'

I glanced at him. 'You don't have breakfast?'

'Never. We cannot afford. School lunch is my only meal.'

'What?' I said. 'No supper either?'

'Just *mamaliga*. Romanian cornmeal mush. We eat big pot of it with salt and butter. Sometimes sour cream if we can afford.'

'It sounds a bit like mushy warm tortilla chips.' I said. 'Non-crunchy nachos. I could live with that.'

'But that is all we have every single night,' he said. 'And then nothing till school lunch. I get so hungry by break time.'

My face felt hot, and not just from the steam. 'So my crisps are your only breakfast?'

'Yes! You are so kind to give them to me.'

I frowned. 'So you *haven't* been mugging me?'

'Of course not.' Dinu slung an arm around my shoulders and squeezed. 'We are friends.'

The steam made it too hot for a bro-hug so I shrugged him off. Then I rounded on him. 'If we're friends, why did you steal my phone?'

He gave a sheepish grin and wiped sweat from his forehead. 'I was coming to say hello, but then I saw phone and wanted to borrow it.'

'So you just borrowed it?'

'Yes. To see what it is like having phone.'

'And then ran away.'

'Yes.'

'That's not borrowing. That's stealing.'

He sighed. The steam had made his dripping face very pink. 'All right. Maybe I did steal. I am sorry. I will give it back.'

'You'll give it back?'

'Yes. When we get home.'

'*If* we get home,' I muttered. 'And if I don't suffocate first.'

'Quickly!' Lollia ran into the steam-room with Plecta close behind. 'Some women are coming.'

'Women are coming!' I translated to Dinu.

But Lollia had already grabbed his hand and was pulling him after her through a thickly curtained arched doorway. 'Hurry!'

My first thought was, Why is Lollia holding HIS hand?

Plecta took my hand and tugged.

My next thought was, Why is Plecta holding MY hand?

'If they find boys in here, they will tear you apart like Pentheus!' said Plecta, her brown eyes wide with fear.

I wasn't sure who Pentheus was but I understood 'tear apart'.

My final thought was, *RUN!*

40
Diana's Garden

The room we ran into was cooler and brighter than the steam-room. It had high glazed windows, a shiny tile floor and it echoed with the sound of slaps and grunts. I saw some female slaves working on the bare backs of women lying on high couches.

'Excellent!' said Dinu. 'Massage room.'

Plecta skidded to a halt and whispered something into the ear of an unoccupied massage-slave. The girl's eyes grew wide and she pointed to another doorway with a curtain.

'This way, Lollia!' called out Plecta, and pulled aside the curtain. Lollia and Dinu skidded to a halt, reversed their direction and followed us along a corridor past a twelve-seater toilet.

The toilet had no dividing walls and no doors! Once again I had to use all my self-control not to look at the women sitting there but to keep my eyes fixed on Lollia. Unfortunately I couldn't shut my nose, so breathed through my mouth as much as possible.

Finally we were out through a squeaky door and into a long and narrow garden, full of dripping green plants. It was raining again, which probably explained why the area was deserted.

I saw a painted statue, stone benches and the windowless back wall of a big square building at the far end of the garden.

'Along the side of that building!' said Lollia.

'No time!' cried Plecta. 'Hide in the bushes!'

The slave-girl shoved the three of us between two bushes and dived in after us. We found ourselves in a narrow space between prickly shrubs and a rough brick wall.

I was amazed at Plecta's boldness and was half expecting Lollia to give her a slap when we heard the squeaky hinge of a door opening followed by women's voices. I couldn't make out what they were saying, but one of them sounded angry. The angry voice was coming closer.

We froze in position: crouched down and huddled together with our knees to our chins and our bottoms on the slightly damp earth. The brick wall was hard against my back and I could feel Plecta's bare arm trembling against mine.

The voices passed us by, heading towards the big building.

One of the shrubs was trying to poke me in the eye, but I didn't dare move. The women might be back any moment.

'What is happening?' whispered Dinu.

'Shhhh!' I breathed in his ear. 'Don't make a noise or we're in deep trouble.'

Dinu shut up. Just in time, as we all heard the voices of the women growing louder as they came back.

Now I felt a sneeze coming! Gran had taught me that a good way to make yourself sneeze is to look at the sky. But I didn't want to sneeze. I wanted the opposite. So I shut my eyes, tipped my head down and pinched my nose.

But it was no good. The sneeze was coming, coming . . .

Ah-brrrrrgh!

The bath-house door slammed at the exact moment of my stifled sneeze, but we all held our breath. We were so quiet that we could hear the sound of rain pattering on the leaves of the bushes and trees around us.

After another five minutes of heart-thudding suspense we reckoned we were safe.

'Well done, Plecta,' breathed Lollia. 'If you hadn't pushed us in here, they might have caught us.'

Plecta actually blushed. Maybe it was the first time her mistress had praised her.

Cautiously we emerged from the bushes. At the centre of the wet and deserted garden was a painted marble statue of a girl in a short tunic with some dogs at her feet. She held a bow in one hand and was reaching towards the quiver on her back with her other.

'Diana,' I said to Dinu. 'Goddess of the hunt.'

He nodded.

Lollia pointed at the blank windowless wall at the far end of the narrow garden. 'That must be a temple to Diana,' she said. 'These baths are hers too, I think.'

'Look,' said Dinu. He held out his hand. It was trembling. 'I am shaking.'

'No wonder,' I said. 'You were fighting to the death less than an hour ago and then you saw a man stab himself and now you've been chased through a bath house full of naked women.'

He looked back at me with his Cleopatra eyes, still wearing Lollia's palla over his head, and then he started to laugh.

'I have not had so much fun in my whole life,' he said.

I stared at him in astonishment. Then I started to laugh too.

'The girls and I walked on the side of London Bridge,' I said, when I could catch my breath, 'singing made-up lyrics to "Greensleeves"!'

'What is "Greensleeves"?' asked Dinu.

This sent me into fresh waves of laughter. I had to hug my sides, I was laughing so hard.

The girls were watching us with open mouths and shining eyes. Then Lollia cupped her hands and whispered something in Plecta's ear. Plecta nodded yes and both girls giggled.

'Dinu!' said Lollia, catching his hand. 'Come sit with me.'

Dinu was still laughing as she pulled him to one of two stone benches set against a wall between shrubs. I was no longer laughing. Once again, I felt a stab of jealousy.

But when Plecta took my hand, I felt the same tingle I had felt on the bridge. Now I was confused.

'Alexandros,' she whispered shyly, 'will you sit with me?'

I let her lead me to the other bench. She kept hold of my hand as we sat.

'Thank you for being so kind to me,' she said. 'It has been a long time since someone treated me as not a slave.'

'I can't believe how cruel she is to you,' I said.

Plecta lowered her eyes and her voice. 'I am afraid of her sometimes . . .'

'Because she beats you and pinches you?'

'Yes, but also because she could do worse things to me.'

'Like what?'

Plecta lowered her voice even more. 'Lollia's mother was a witch, and she is one too. She has a secret dog-tooth to prove it.'

'A what?'

Plecta pointed to her own mouth. 'An extra tooth here, behind her dog-tooth.'

I stared at her in horror. Lollia had a dog-tooth? Then I remembered the word 'canine' meant dog. But having an extra tooth was still creepy.

Plecta brought her lips close to my ear. 'Lollia's mother

left her a box of magic herbs and spices. She does midnight magic sometimes.'

Plecta's words made me shiver. Or maybe it was her warm breath in my ear. I turned and looked at her.

With her big chocolate-coloured eyes and gently parted lips, she seemed almost as beautiful as her mistress. And way nicer.

'Will you tell me about yourself, Plecta?' I said.

'Yes,' she said, 'I will tell you.'

41
Plecta of Pergamum

'I grew up in a town called Pergamum,' said Plecta, 'far away in Asia. My parents were not rich but they were well off and respected in the city. My father made parchment like his father before him, and his father and all the way back to Attalus. It was a respected business with a shop in the lower agora and a workshop down by the Temple of the Healer. But then the plague came.'

'The same plague that Lollia told me about?'

'Yes. It killed everyone in my family except me and my little sister, and a distant cousin named Cleophon. He took all my father's possessions and sold me and my sister to a slave-dealer.'

'You were his cousins, and he *sold* you?' Of all the things I had seen and heard so far, this was the worst.

Plecta inclined her head to say yes. 'My first mistress owned a troupe of acrobats whose job was to perform for her every evening. My sister was with me, so it was like being in a big family with aunts and uncles. That is where I learned to dance and walk on a tightrope. But then our mistress died and the troupe was sold to an ex-soldier. He didn't want the younger members, so he sold me and my sister to a slave-dealer in Massilia. That is when Lollia's father bought me, so I could nurse her back to health when she had fever. And there is another reason.'

She brought her mouth close to my ear. 'When I first met Lollia, she had horse-rider's legs and walked with a limp.'

I was confused. 'What are horse-rider's legs?'

'Like you are riding a horse, with your knees apart. But now she is very graceful, as you saw on the bridge.'

I said, 'Did you ever see your sister again?'

Plecta lifted her chin to say no. 'I will never see her again, I think. My family is gone and I am alone.'

'What will happen to you when Lollia gets married?' I asked.

Plecta dropped her head so I could not see her face. 'I will go with her. I am part of her dowry. I pray her husband's family treats me kindly.'

'You're going to live with them?'

'Yes. His family is rich and Lollia's father thinks it is a good match. But she does not want to marry him.'

'What about you?' I asked. 'If you could have any life, what would it be?'

Plecta gazed out into the green garden. 'I loved being part of the troupe,' she said. 'It was like a big family. I would like that again. If I joined a troupe of acrobats then maybe I would marry one who had all his teeth and good skin like you. We would buy our freedom and have many babies. I would also like to return to Asia where it is warm and not always muddy and wet.'

I took a deep breath. 'What would happen to you if Lollia died?' I asked.

She automatically made the sign against evil and whispered, 'I do not know.'

We both looked over towards Lollia, and my jaw dropped. She was kissing Dinu!

42
Salsa Mouse

L ater – much later – I found out about TTLS or 'Tittles'. TTLS stands for 'Time Travellers' Love Syndrome'.

It's similar to when people survive an earthquake or some other near-death experience. As soon as they know they're not going to die, they often fall into each other's arms in relief.

But at that moment in the Gardens of Diana, I had no idea how time travel was affecting us.

All I knew was that it was a terrible idea to be getting involved with girls who lived hundreds of years ago and whom we would never see again.

'Dinu!' I hissed. 'You can't kiss Lollia. We're not supposed to interact, remember?' I was speaking in English of course.

'Is too late for that,' said Dinu. 'Anyway, I really like her. I want to bring her back with us.'

'WHAT?'

He gave a lopsided grin and shrugged. 'She can be girlfriend.'

'Dinu, you can't bring her back.' I tried to think of a way to put him off. 'She has terrible teeth and bad breath.'

'I have plan. I will take her to free NHS dentist. They will fix her teeth and make her beautiful.'

'She has bandy legs.'

'I do not care.'

'Dinu, she's a witch. She has an extra tooth in her mouth and a box of magic herbs at her house. Plecta told me.'

'Plecta is jealous because Lollia is very beautiful.'

'Lollia may be beautiful, but Plecta is brave and good. Anyway, you can't bring someone back through the time portal. Solomon Daisy said so.'

'Who is Solomon Daisy?'

'The bazillionaire whose tech guys invented the time machine.'

The girls were looking at us with frowns. They had heard their names but had no idea what we were saying.

'How do they know you cannot bring person back?' said Dinu. 'Has anyone tried?'

'Yes,' I said. 'This boy named Martin – I met him before I came here. He was the first one to go through the portal.'

'Someone went back in time before us?'

'Yes, but he was too scared to leave the Mithraeum. While he was in there,' I continued, 'he made friends with a little mouse and decided to bring it back as an experiment.'

'What happened to mouse?' asked Dinu.

'It exploded into chunky salsa.'

Dinu narrowed his eyes, almost like he didn't believe me.

Of course he was right not to believe me.

'Salsa Mouse' was a total lie.

'I can tell you are lying, Wimpy,' said Dinu, 'because you make eyes wide like baby.'

I only had one argument left and this one was going to hurt. I took a deep breath. 'Here's the thing, Dinu,' I said. 'You can't bring her back because she's going to die soon.'

I have heard people say 'white as a sheet', but he actually went white as a sheet. 'Lollia will die soon?' He looked at her in disbelief and she looked back, puzzled.

'I'm sorry . . . but yes. It's her fate to die aged fourteen.'

He put his arm around her shoulders. 'Then we must bring her back more than ever!'

'No!' I cried. 'That would definitely cause a time crash! If we bring Lollia back to our time to stop her from dying, then the archaeologists never would have found her bones and Solomon Daisy wouldn't have become obsessed and he would never have sent us back . . .'

Dinu was just staring at me.

My head was beginning to throb again and I felt sick.

'What's wrong?' asked Lollia, looking from me to Dinu and back to me. 'What are you two talking about? Why do you have that look on your face?'

'I feel a bit sick,' I said to her in Greek. 'I think I need the latrine.' It was partly true. I'd assumed because I hadn't touched a bite of food in nearly four days I wouldn't need the loo. I was wrong.

'Go in the bushes where we hid,' said Plecta, also looking worried. 'Do you want me to stand guard?'

'No,' I said. 'You wait here. I'll be right back.' Then in English to Dinu, 'I'm just using the bushes as a toilet. Don't go anywhere.'

I pushed the wet shrubs aside and found the place where we had crouched earlier.

Maybe I shouldn't have bothered to dig a little hole with a twig.

Maybe I shouldn't have searched around for the perfect leaves to wipe with.

Maybe I shouldn't have taken the time to carefully cover it all over again and pat the damp earth down on top.

Because when I emerged from my leafy latrine, Plecta was standing alone by the benches, wringing her hands.

Dinu and Lollia were nowhere to be seen.

43
Blind Love

'They left me!' Plecta stood in the rain, her chin trembling. 'She told me I couldn't come.'

'Where?' I cried. 'Where did they go?'

'I think Dinu said something about the Cave of Mithras, but she said they should go to the basilica first.' She was twisting her hands together. 'She abandoned me!'

'Oh no!' I breathed. 'He'll try to take her to our land and she'll die!'

Plecta burst into tears. 'I will also die!' she cried. 'They will think I killed her and ran away. They crucify runaway slaves.'

My stomach did a somersault and my skin prickled all over.

She threw her arms around me and sobbed. 'Alexandros, you have to find her!'

I hugged her back for a moment, mainly because I felt dizzy too. Then I gently pushed her away.

'We'll find her,' I said. 'Do you know how to find the Cave of Mithras?'

'No.' Plecta was shivering and her teeth were chattering. 'We have never been north of the river before.'

'Of course you haven't.' My mind was spinning like the front wheel of a bicycle doing a wheelie: it couldn't get a grip on anything. I gently banged the side my head with the heel of my hand. 'Think, Alex!' I said. 'Think!'

I tried to visualise the map of Londinium I had memorised.

I knew the bridge we had crossed went straight on to the basilica, and that the Mithraeum was down to the left, south-west from there. But when we had run away from Lollia's fiancé we had got all confused.

But the basilica was the biggest building in Londinium, even bigger than the amphitheatre. If I could spot that, I would be able to get my bearings.

I looked around, but the Temple of Diana loomed up on our right and the trees of the narrow garden blocked my view in other directions.

'Come on,' I said. 'We need to get out on the street so I can see where we are.'

At the end of the narrow garden was an even narrower alley. The alley ended at a tall wooden gate with its bar on the inside. The wooden bar had not quite fallen back into its cradle.

'They must have come this way,' I said. But as I started to lift the bar, Plecta stopped me with a touch. 'My mistress and your slave changed tunics before they went, so we had better become ourselves again too,' she said.

We turned our backs on each other and quickly switched back to our own tunics.

When I turned back I saw Plecta fixing her twisted-up hair in place with a bone hairpin. 'If we cannot find them, will you protect me?' Her chocolate-brown eyes were brimming with tears and her lower lip trembled.

'Yes,' I said with more confidence than I felt. I remembered the crucified man at the crossroads and tried not to shudder.

I lifted the beam of the inner gate, opened it a little and peeked out. It led into a busy street with men and women and litters moving both ways. When I was sure nobody was looking, I stepped out. Plecta pulled her palla over her head and shoulders. Then she followed me out, careful to step with her right foot first.

I made sure to leave the gate slightly ajar in case we needed a quick escape route later on.

The moment we stepped out onto the street, the sun came out from behind a cloud and shone down on bolts of coloured fabric and bunches of dyed wool outside the shops on the other side of the street. That explained why there were more women here than I had seen anywhere else in Londinium; this was a cloth market.

The altar of the temple and its entrance were on our right. Further along, at the end of the road, I saw a good omen. It was still raining there, and the sun made a rainbow that ended at the red-tiled roof of a building rising up above all the other buildings. It was Londinium's great basilica. *Thank you, God!* I prayed.

'Come on!' I urged, tugging Plecta's hand.

'We must not run,' she hissed, 'or people will notice us. Only thieves and robbers run,' she added. 'Also,' she said, 'only those who are married or engaged hold hands.'

So we walked as fast as we dared, keeping our heads down.

'Why would they go to the basilica?' I asked as we went.

'I don't know,' she said. 'Her father goes there to do business sometimes. Maybe she wants to introduce Dinu to him.'

'We've got to stop them,' I muttered. 'Dinu has to come back with me.'

'Why?' she asked. 'Why must you go?'

'We have to go back to our country,' I said. 'We both have family there.'

'You're lucky,' she said. 'You have a family.'

'Yes,' I said. I looked at her and felt a wave of sorrow for her hard life. I wondered how long she had to live. Her mistress would be talked about hundreds of years in the future but no one would ever know what happened to her slave-girl.

'How old are you, Plecta?' I asked.

'Twelve years, eleven months and twenty days,' she said. 'On the Kalends I will be thirteen.'

'Does everyone here know their exact age?' I asked.

'Of course. Each day we are allowed to look upon the light of day is a gift from the gods. *Memento mori*,' she added in Latin. 'Remember that you must die.'

'*Carpe diem*,' I said softly. 'Seize the moment!' And even though we were not betrothed, she let me hold her hand.

44

Indoor Pigeons

Remember I told you about the Tate Modern, that big art gallery by the River Thames? It used to be a power station and there is still a room called the Turbine Hall. If you want an idea of how high the roof of the ancient basilica was, go to the lowest part of the Turbine Hall at the Tate Modern and then look up.

I don't know if the dimensions were exactly the same, but it felt very similar.

London's basilica was humongous.

There were pigeons flying around up there and everything. The afternoon sun sent beams slanting down through high arched windows. Where they hit the floor I could see it was made of coloured marble. Plecta and I stood open-mouthed. Then some pigeon poop splattered on the expensive floor just in front of us, so we closed our mouths and reminded ourselves we were there to find Lollia and Dinu.

'Let's make our way to the other end and see if we can spot them,' I said to Plecta. She inclined her head in agreement. As we started towards the far end of the giant building, she took my hand again.

Holding Plecta's hand felt reassuring and scary at the same time. Reassuring because it meant she cared about me as much as I did about her. Scary because if they couldn't find Lollia they would torture Plecta to find out what she knew. And that would be my fault.

The basilica wasn't too busy. I remembered that Romans tended to work in the mornings and go to the baths or relax in the afternoon. Also, I had read somewhere that business wasn't usually conducted on days when the games were on. But maybe the citizens of Londinium hadn't got that memo.

I could see there was a better class of person here. About a third of the men were dressed like Epapras, in cream-coloured togas over tunics with two vertical red stripes on them. I guessed it was the ancient equivalent of a suit and tie. Because they all wore the same uniform, you could easily compare one to another and tell the high-quality fabric from the cheap stuff. One guy's tunic was so thin that you could almost see through it.

There were almost no women or children in here.

The only kids our age were standing quietly by a veiled woman while a man in a toga spoke to some men on benches. The toga man was waving his arms a lot and he kept gesturing at the woman and her kids. I guessed he was a lawyer pleading her case. There were a few other cases in session, but because the roof was so high they didn't drown each other out. Each lawyer stood near a niche in the wall and addressed men on benches with their backs to the central aisle. There were also some raised blocks of marble, or maybe marble covered brick, with a man sitting on each one where a case was being argued. I guessed the men on the blocks were judges and the people on the benches were like modern juries. The defendants – the people on trial – usually stood to one side looking miserable.

Once we passed a pair of almost-naked men with bruises on their bodies and metal chains around their ankles. When one of them turned I saw his back was raw and bloody where he had been whipped.

I could feel Plecta's hand trembling in mine. She said in a low voice, 'Runaway slaves.'

I shuddered too, remembering the crucified man I had seen at the crossroads that morning.

Suddenly Plecta's fingers tightened on mine.

'There they are!' she said. 'I see them!'

Lollia and Dinu stood by a niche in the wall facing each other, right hands clasped like when you shake hands. A golden beam of sunlight fell on them and seemed to make their blond hair glow, almost as if they had halos.

I had to admit they were a good-looking couple.

Coming closer, I saw a statue of a naked woman in the niche behind them and guessed it was Venus, the goddess of love. Four men in togas stood nearby, watching Dinu and Lollia intently. The youngest was fluffy-bearded Epapras.

'Oh no!' cried Plecta. 'I think they are getting married!'

'Where's the priest?' I said.

She gave me a puzzled look. 'They don't need a priest,' she said. 'They only need to hold hands and make a vow in the presence of witnesses.'

'Stop!' cried a voice behind me. 'Stop that ceremony!'

I turned to see the fat bald man in a striped tunic from earlier jogging towards us. Behind him came a distinguished-looking man with silver-blond hair and two soldiers.

'*Eheu!*' cried Plecta. Alas! 'Tertius has found us. And he's brought Lollia's father!'

'Dinu, run!' I shouted in English. 'Head back to the Mithraeum! They're going to arrest you!'

Dinu looked around, startled. His eyes widened when he saw me, then widened even more at the sight of two soldiers bearing down on him.

Lollia and Dinu looked at each other and then ran, still holding hands. Fluffy-bearded Epapras charged after them, his toga flapping. Plecta and I looked at each other and without a word we ran, too.

Suddenly, with a cry of '*Pesta toga!*' Epapras tripped on his toga and sprawled onto the marble floor of the great basilica.

Plecta skidded to a halt. 'Are you all right, sir?' she asked him in Greek.

'Yes,' he groaned. 'Only my dignity is bruised.' He gazed up at her. 'Your Greek is excellent,' he said. 'Are you by any chance from Pergamum?'

Plecta gave the downward nod for yes and I bent forward to help him up, but he waved us on.

'Go! Go!' he cried. 'I'll try to delay them for you.'

'Thank you, sir,' said Plecta.

I grabbed her hand and together we ran out into a massive forum.

The rain clouds had gone and it was a beautiful afternoon. We were just in time to see Dinu and Lollia weaving between market stalls towards the western exit, back the way we had come.

The stalls here were the biggest and most luxurious of any I had seen so far. Lots of them displayed those big clay jars full of wine or maybe olive oil. In fact we almost ran into a half-naked slave with a huge amphora on his shoulder but managed to dodge around him.

Once outside the forum and back on the road, we looked around for the runaway lovebirds.

Plecta pointed. 'There they are!'

I caught a flash of Lollia's blue palla and loose golden hair as they headed north.

'That's not the way to the Mithraeum,' I said. 'They're going in the opposite direction!'

45
House-Tombs

Thanks to Lollia's sapphire-blue palla and Dinu's height, we managed to keep them in sight. They skirted the western side of the forum and then veered right to run along the imposing northern wall of the basilica. There was a kind of industrial area here, with workshops. We passed several potteries, a glassmaker and, by the smell of it, a pee-laundry.

We were still running, even though I was pretty sure we had shaken off our pursuers. Once I stepped in a cowpat and nearly slipped on my flat leather soles, but by then we were in sight of the lofty town walls and twin arched gates, so we slowed to a walk and tried to look casual. Later on I found it was Bishopsgate. In my time there would be a massive gherkin-shaped skyscraper here.

There were soldiers on guard duty, but they looked bored. One was talking to the driver of a cart coming through the right-hand gate and the other was watching some boys who were rolling a hoop near a cheese stall.

'I don't see Lollia or Dinu anywhere,' I said.

'I think they went through the gate,' panted Plecta, 'into the cemetery. Lollia needs the spirits of the dead to help her with her magic spells.'

'She's doing magic *now*?'

Plecta tipped her head for yes. We were walking as fast as we could without seeming to hurry. Would the soldiers stop the twenty-first century boy and possible runaway slave-girl?

They didn't even look at us.

As we went through the left-hand gate I saw dozens of small altars under the arch on both sides of the road. A man was lighting a candle at one of them. A line of bricks in the gravel road showed where Londinium ended and its northern graveyard began. I was careful to step over with my right foot.

Then we were back out into daylight, into the cemetery. I shivered as I remembered the Greek word for graveyard. It's *necropolis*, which means 'city of the dead'.

And that's exactly what the cemetery looked like. The road was lined with buildings that were homes for the dead rather than the living.

My dad is buried in Brompton Cemetery, where there are lots of similar house-tombs, called mausoleums. The difference between this cemetery and Brompton Cemetery

was that there were no trees here, only a few little shrubs. I suddenly realised why I kept seeing carts full of wood. Once there had been vast forests of ancient oak trees surrounding London, but three hundred years of heating bath houses, burning bodies and offering up burnt sacrifices had used up all the wood for miles around.

No trees meant there was nothing but mud and weeds around the tombs, apart from little bumps where cremation urns stuck up out of the ground.

Unlike Brompton Cemetery, which is usually deserted when I go there with Gran, I could see movement everywhere. Beggars huddled by a house-tomb close to where the great wall of the city rose up on my left. Mourners stood around a smoking pyre a hundred metres to the north-west. Feral dogs prowled about too, looking for something to eat. Wheeled traffic moved both ways on the road, which I found out later was called Ermine Street.

Then I spotted Dinu peeping out from behind a mausoleum on the right-hand side of the road. The top of the mausoleum had a painted stone sculpture of a lion devouring a stag.

Instead of ducking out of sight or running away as I expected, Dinu beckoned us over.

Plecta and I looked at each other and jogged along a footpath beside the road, in order to avoid cowpats, donkey dung and several mule-drawn carts heading our way.

'Dinu!' I hissed when I we reached the lion tomb. 'What are you doing?'

'She told me to keep watch,' he said. 'You were right. She is witch and doing something like magic. Are they still chasing us?'

I shook my head, then asked, 'Can you actually understand her?'

'Little bit,' he said. 'When she speaks Latin. Is not so different from Romanian, you know.'

I looked around for Lollia but couldn't see her. Then Plecta pointed and I caught a glint of her fair hair. She was sitting on the ground behind a grave marker near a bush.

I tiptoed towards Lollia, trying to be as quiet as I could.

As I got closer I heard her speaking in a strange sing-song voice, like when people talk to a baby or a pet. Her head was bent over something, but I couldn't see what it was.

Curiosity drew me closer. Plecta followed, as silent as a ghost.

When I was finally close enough to see, I managed not to gasp in horror.

Lollia held a little beeswax figure of a pot-bellied man. He had copper needles in his eyes, mouth and tummy button, like a voodoo doll.

She was using her ivory leopard knife to cut off his feet.

46
Roman Voodoo

'She made that figure yesterday at midnight,' Plecta murmured in my ear. 'We did it in a graveyard near us.'

It was strange to think Plecta and Lollia had been awake under those stars too. Doing black magic.

'Do you do it too?' I asked quietly.

She tipped her head back for no. 'I kept watch. Magic frightens me. She summons spirits of the dead to be her messengers. She does not want to marry Tertius the brewer.'

'Is that wax doll supposed to be him?'

'Yes,' said Plecta. 'She found some of his hairs, though he does not have very many, and put them in. Also pits from olives he had eaten and dregs from the bottom of his wine cup. She is trying to make him sick so she will not have to marry him.'

'Why did she tie a twig to his back?'

'That is not a twig. I think it is someone's finger bone.'

Lollia must have heard me gasp. Her head jerked around and she looked up at us. She reminded me of a blue-eyed leopard disturbed in the middle of devouring its prey.

Then she turned back to her singing and sawing.

At that moment I realised that Lollia was not like the Mean Girls at my school. She was a creature from another time, another world, another mindset.

I shuddered.

Plecta murmured in my ear. 'When she made that figure she also chanted a summoning spell to bring a new betrothed. This morning when we heard that a beautiful boy was looking for a blue-eyed girl with ivory knife she was convinced her magic had worked.'

'Me,' I breathed.

'And then Dinu,' said Plecta. 'She is convinced she has power.'

Once again I shuddered. Solomon Daisy had said his time portal was *non magia, sed scientia*. But I wondered: did magic and science ever attract each other, like magnets?

Suddenly all our heads went up at the sound of a man's voice calling out, 'Lollia, are you here?'

'Alas!' whispered Lollia, and she was suddenly human again. 'It is my father!'

47
Daddy's Girl

Lollia dropped the little voodoo figure into the open mouth of a clay jar half buried in the ground. All three of us ran to the nearest mausoleum and pressed ourselves against the wall.

'Lollia! Please!' came his voice. 'It's dangerous out here. There are robbers and kidnappers.'

A moment later Dinu joined the three of us. 'Her father is here,' he panted in my ear. 'I think he is alone.'

'Dinu says he's alone,' I translated.

Lollia frowned, put her finger to her lips and peeked out. Then she ran towards the road.

What happened next surprised us all. Lollia hugged her father.

'Pater, I'm sorry!' she cried. 'It's just that I can't bear to marry Tertius. Please may I marry Dionysus instead?'

'Dionysus?' cried her father.

They had been speaking Greek, but Dinu must have heard his name, because he ran to them, *'Ego sum Dionysus!'* he cried.

'Who are you and where are you from?' Lollia's father asked him, also in Latin.

Dinu did not reply, and when Lollia tried to speak for him her father silenced her with a gesture.

'Who are you and where are you from?' This time Lollia's father spoke in Greek, but of course Dinu did not understand.

I took a deep breath and stepped out from behind the tomb. 'Dionysus is my slave,' I said in my best olive-vowel Greek. 'We have just arrived in Londinium from a faraway land.'

Lollia's father looked from me to Plecta and back to me. 'Who are you? Why is the slave-girl with you and not attending my daughter?'

'My name is Alexandros son of Philippos. My slave and I were shipwrecked and escaped with only our lives. Your daughter and her slave-girl were kind enough to help us. Lollia redeemed my slave after he was sold to the gladiator school.'

Lollia's father looked Dinu up and down. I could see him taking in his blond hair, clear skin and muscular body but also his unbelted blue tunic and lack of shoes. 'I can see he's a fine specimen, but a slave . . . ?' Marcus Lollius

Honoratus turned to his daughter. 'You would marry an illiterate slave with no possessions? What on earth are you thinking?'

Lollia buried her face in her father's cloak. 'Please don't make me marry Tertius. He's fat and bald and his breath smells of beer.'

Honoratus stood stiffly for a moment. Then he patted his daughter's back. 'Lollia,' he said, 'if you hate Tertius so much then I can find you another husband. But not that boy. He doesn't even speak Greek. Is there nobody else you would take for a husband?'

Lollia wiped her face on her palla and looked up at her father. 'Maybe Petros?' she said in a small voice.

'Petros the glassmaker's son?'

Lollia gave a single downward nod. 'He has nice eyes and he always smiles at me.'

'When did you speak to him? Or even meet him?'

'He has been to our house twice with his father to show you their glassware.'

'What's happening?' Dinu asked me in English.

'She's asking her father if she can marry the glassmaker's son instead of the pub owner,' I said.

'What about me?' whispered Dinu. 'Doesn't she want to marry me?'

'Yes, but her father won't hear of her marrying someone who can't speak Greek or Latin.'

Lollia reached down the front of her tunic and pulled out a little blue glass bottle. 'Petros gave me this miniature amphora of clove oil for my tooth. He told me it comes all the way from Greece,' she added.

Her father gave a big sigh. 'Very well,' he said. 'You may marry Petros if his father agrees to the match.'

Lollia hung her head. 'Thank you, Pater.'

'But you must promise to never run away again. This town is no place for a girl on her own.'

She inclined her head for yes and threw her arms around him. Her father hugged her back and kissed the top of her tousled blonde head.

'Oh no,' said Dinu.

'Don't feel bad,' I said. 'You know we can't stay.'

He hung his head like a beaten dog. 'I know. Can I maybe say goodbye?'

I nodded. 'Sir,' I said to Lollia's father in Greek, 'I will take my slave and go. But may he say farewell to your daughter?'

Lollia looked up at Honoratus. 'Please, Father?' she said. 'Can I just say goodbye to him?'

Her father gave a single downward nod of assent. 'But let us leave this ill-omened place,' he said, making the sign against evil and spitting on the ground. 'You may speak to each other until we reach the town gate.' As Dinu stretched out his hand Lollia's father added sharply, 'You may not touch each other. That would be scandalous.'

So Dinu and Lollia walked back side by side in the late afternoon light, almost but not quite touching.

Plecta and I followed behind, walking on the path between tombs and road. Marcus Lollius Honoratus brought up the rear. It wasn't far to the twin arches of the gate, only a few hundred paces, but it was enough for me to tell Plecta that I thought she was brave and good. I prayed she would one day gain her freedom and have a family.

Up ahead, I thought I saw Lollia give Dinu something, but it was so quick that I couldn't be sure.

When we reached the entrance arch of Londinium's gate we were all careful to step over the boundary with our right foot first. Once inside and past the guards, we stopped beside a stall selling great wheels of yellow cheese.

'I hope you reach your home safely, Alexandros,' said Plecta. 'I will make an offering to Venus on your behalf every day of my life.' Her eyes were brimming with tears.

I had been trying to think of some secret I could give her that might make her rich or at least help her gain her freedom. Suddenly I had it.

'Pockets!' I cried in English. And in Greek, 'You could invent them! You'd become rich!'

Instead of asking me what a 'pocket' was, Plecta was looking past me with horrified eyes.

'Oh no!' she said. 'The lanista is coming this way. I think he regrets letting Dinu go.'

I turned to see the mafia-type lanista stalking towards us, flanked by two of his fiercest gladiators; one had a trident and the other one waved a sword.

'Dinu!' I yelled in English. 'No more time for goodbyes! Run!'

48
Chickens on a Tray

We found the door in the wall of the Mithraeum villa easily enough. It was south-west of the massive basilica, east of the Walbrook stream. The only problem was that it was guarded by a man wearing a dark brown tunic and a raven mask.

'That can't be good,' muttered Dinu.

'Get back!' I pulled him back into the alley where we were hiding. 'I need to think. They must be having a ceremony.'

A few moments later a skinny guy in a pale blue tunic trotted past the mouth of our alleyway, heading for the Mithraeum villa. He was carrying a stack of round loaves bound with twine, holding them in front of his torso like a man playing an accordion.

'He has tunic like ours,' said Dinu.

I looked at the tunics Dinu and I were wearing. They were pale blue linen, the same colour and fabric as the tunics of the slaves who had chased us when we first left the Mithraeum. I had not seen anyone else wearing a tunic this colour. I realised they must be a kind of uniform worn only by the slaves of the Mithraeum villa.

As we watched, Bread Boy went straight through the open door into the villa garden.

'They must be having an initiation,' I said. 'With a feast afterwards. I bet there will be lots of slaves bringing food to prepare the meal. I have an idea of how we can get in. But we need money. Do you have anything we can sell?'

Dinu looked at a gold ring on the little finger of his left hand. 'I have only this,' he said. 'But I cannot give away. See? It has grapes of Dionysus – for good luck.'

'Where did you get that?'

'Lollia gave it to me for keepsake, because my name Dinu is from Dionysus.'

'Dinu,' I said, 'don't you know the first rule of time travel? *Naked you go, and naked you must return!* Take it off.'

'I don't think I can. Is stuck.'

'You have to take it off,' I said. 'Otherwise when we go back through the time portal, the metal will explode and you'll lose a finger or maybe your whole hand.'

'I need soap,' he said. 'Soap will make it slippery.'

'I'm pretty sure they don't have soap in Roman times,' I said. 'They used olive oil instead.'

'Then olive oil.'

'Olive oil costs a fortune, and we don't have time to find any. In fact, we don't really have time at all.'

Two more slaves in blue tunics were passing us. One had a couple of big wine-skins, one over each shoulder. The other held a wooden tray of live chickens on his head. The chickens sat calmly, not fussing and not even clucking. In fact they were so relaxed that one right on the edge fell off and plopped onto the muddy road. Its feet were tied, which explained why it did not run away and also why all the other chickens had been sitting so obediently.

'This is our chance!' I hissed to Dinu. 'Follow my lead and don't say anything.'

I rushed forward and picked up the muddy white hen. The two slaves had turned around. '*Adsumus adiuvare!*' I said, which I hoped meant, 'We are here to help.'

The slaves stared stupidly at us. One of them was cross-eyed and the other one's mouth hung open. I could almost read their minds: we were wearing the livery of the Mithraeum villa, but they had never seen us before.

'Dinu, take one of the wine-skins,' I muttered out of the side of my mouth.

Dinu tried to take one of the wine-skins from the cross-eyed slave, but he would not let go.

'*Festinate!*' I told them, with all the confidence I could muster. Hurry!

They looked at each other and shrugged.

The one with the wine-skins let Dinu help.

Dinu and I followed them towards the door in the wall, me carrying the single chicken under my arm and Dinu with one of the heavy wine-skins.

Praise the gods! Another slave in a pale blue tunic waved us through.

We were in the grounds of the Mithraeum villa! Now we only needed to get into the Mithraeum itself.

There was only one problem. They were obviously about to have one of their ceremonies, followed by the famous ritual dinner I had read about. If there were men inside the temple, then how could we even get in?

Underneath the tall tree I saw a food preparation area like for a big barbecue. There were tables and stools and a firepit and about a dozen slaves in blue tunics chopping, plucking, mixing and cooking. One was even turning a pig on a spit. A stocky man in a long orange tunic and matching turban was supervising them. I recognised him as the one who had shouted at us the day before. Would he recognise us again? For the moment he had his back to us. But he could turn and spot us at any moment.

Over to the right was the Mithraeum. Its double front doors were firmly closed and the man with the raven mask nowhere to be seen. The ceremony must have started. But I remembered the two glassless windows in the dressing room. I could see them in the plaster outer wall of the building. They weren't too high because the Mithraeum was partly sunk. And the drop on the other side was not too bad, especially if Dinu went in first and helped me through.

'Come on, Dinu!' I hissed, putting down my chicken. 'This might be our only chance to get inside.'

49
Flight Simulator

Fortuna, the goddess of luck, was with us. Just a few minutes later we were hiding behind a stone altar near the entrance of the Mithraeum, spying on their secret ceremony. The changing room had been deserted and the inner double doors open. It was almost as if the universe was helping us get back to our own time.

The Mithraeum was full of candlelight, incense and the sound of chanting.

For a moment it felt like the Greek Orthodox church of St Nektarios in Battersea. But only for a moment.

The men's chanting was not like any hymn I'd ever heard in church.

The pungent smell of burning pine cones made me dizzy.

And the damp space felt more like a cave than a church.

The flickering flames of candles, torches and oil lamps showed me things I had not noticed the first time: painted altars here at the back of the temple, frescoes on the walls beyond the columns and even the colours of the columns. The first pair of columns had been painted black, presumably for the lowest level, the Ravens. The next pair of columns was yellow, then a reddish-orange pair, then red, then white, gold and purple.

There were about forty men standing in the two side aisles, chanting. They wore cloaks of the same colours as the columns and a few wore animal masks on their heads. In the flickering light of torches the empty eyeholes made them look extra-creepy.

The only person in the central part of the temple near the time portal was a grey-haired man dressed as Mithras. He wore a long-sleeved tunic, a purple cape and a floppy Smurf-style hat. He held a sword in his right hand and a candle in his left.

I guessed he was the *Pater*, the Father or head priest. He was the only one not chanting.

I had been trying to pick out words from the chant but soon I realised they were only singing vowel sounds, saying '*Aahh, eh, ayyy, eeee, oh, oooh, ohhh . . .*' Some were also shaking the Egyptian rattles Martin had mentioned or clashing little finger cymbals.

'This is strange,' said Dinu in my ear.

'You're telling me!' I replied.

'How do we get to portal?' said Dinu. 'I cannot even see it.'

228

'It's about two metres in front of the Mithras statue,' I replied. 'Keep an eye out for a faint glow or shimmer, like a giant soap bubble blower. I just hope it's dark enough in here for us to see when it comes on.'

'And then?'

'Take off your clothes and make a dash for it,' I said.

Then we had to be quiet, because a horn blared, the worshippers fell silent and the priest dressed as Mithras raised the sword and the candle.

'*Nama, coracibus; tutela Mercurii*,' he chanted. Hail! O ravens, protected by Mercury.

The chorus of caws that greeted this almost made me jump out of my tunic. Some kind of amplifier in the masks left my ears ringing.

'*Nama patri*,' all the men responded, '*tutela Saturni*.' Hail to the father, protected by Saturn.

I nodded in admiration. They had got that part absolutely right at London's twenty-first-century Mithraeum.

And it confirmed the man dressed as Mithras was the Father or *Pater*.

After each of the seven categories had been greeted and the response given, the Father held up his hands with the sword and the candle.

'*Death*,' he said in slow, clear Latin, '*comes to all of us sooner or later. On that day our souls will leave our bodies and rise up to the highest heavens.*'

As if by magic, or maybe a hidden pulley, the candle left his hand and rose up to the ceiling. Dinu gasped and grabbed my wrist. He and I and everyone else looked up and saw about two dozen candles burning like stars against a background of painted constellations. It looked like a planetarium.

'How do they do that?' whispered Dinu.

'Hidden strings?' I said. But it was only a guess.

'Our eternal souls are made of star stuff,' said the Father. *'And to the stars they long to return.'*

He continued talking, and although I couldn't understand every word I got the sense of it. When your soul reached the highest sphere, he said, you would be higher than men and angels and many other spirits. Together with your fellow star-souls, you could look down and see everything: past, present and future.

For a moment I forgot about the portal. Maybe it was the effect of the pine-cone incense or the fact that I had not eaten in over three days, but I was totally absorbed in what he was saying.

I remembered the awesome stars I had seen my first night in Roman London. Was it less than twenty-four hours ago? It would be wonderful to be a star-soul. You would no longer feel hunger or fear or the pain of losing people you loved. It would be amazing to fly through time and space, watching great battles from the past and seeing people colonise planets in the future.

It was my turn to grab Dinu's arm.

'It's not a driving simulator,' I hissed. 'It's a flight simulator!'

'What?' Dinu frowned at me.

'Solomon Daisy told me that going into the Mithraeum was like a driving simulator for the soul. But it's more like a flight simulator – or even one for space flight – so the soul knows where to go when you die.'

Dinu nodded, gazing up in wonder. The candlelight reflected in his blue eyes made them seem green.

I turned my attention back to the Father.

He was saying that, after a few thousand years, being a star-soul would get lonely. You would long to talk to people and discuss the things you had seen. You would miss the feel of winning a race or giving a good speech or holding your newborn child.

That was when your star-soul would go back down through the spheres, longing to get into anything hot-blooded that could smell and taste and feel.

And that was why ordeals must be suffered here on earth, continued the Father, to ensure that the soul will be pure enough to be reborn as a high-born man rather than a bean or an animal.

That was when they brought out the naked man.

50

Torches Up

Two guys with torches, also dressed as Persians with the floppy Smurf hats and short capes, came into the central nave. They were followed by a pair of men in raven masks leading the naked man. I call him that but strictly speaking he wasn't completely naked: he wore a sack over his head and the tiniest loincloth around his waist. His hands were tied behind his back. I could tell he was young because his skin was smooth and hairless.

The Father said something, and suddenly everybody roared like lions. I nearly had a heart attack.

Now the worshippers were doing a strange kind of noisy fast breathing, in and out through their noses.

For a moment silence fell like a blanket on the Mithraeum. Then everyone started hissing and – as if that wasn't weird enough – making popping sounds, using their tongue in their cheeks. I have never heard anything like that before and hope

I never do again. It made all the little hairs on my neck and arms stand up.

At last it was time for the initiation. This is what Mithras-scholars had been waiting centuries to discover.

The Ravens pushed the naked guy forward. He fell to his knees, his hands still tied behind his back and the sack on his head. Torches held by the Persian helpers threw his giant wobbling shadow up onto one of the pillars. The Father came closer, his face lit spookily from below, like when you shine a torch under your chin at Halloween. He still held the sword in one hand, the metal glinting in the flickering light.

The Ravens pulled off the sack to let the naked guy see the sword, before putting the sack back over his head.

The Father addressed the naked guy in a low voice. The naked guy bowed his head as if in assent.

I wasn't the only one who gasped as the Father took a step forward and pulled back his sword.

Dinu was gripping my wrist so hard that it hurt.

The torch-bearers moved closer, holding their torches up. Their fluttering capes hid the stabbing from sight, but when they stood back the naked guy stood facing the Father with his back to us. The sword was stuck right through him, from side to side, and blood dripped down his legs, from both the entry and exit wounds.

Now all the worshippers were making the strange hissing noise again.

One of the torch-bearers went to one side of the statue of Mithras and held his torch up. Naked Guy, somehow still alive, staggered up the steps and disappeared behind the statue of Mithras on the bull.

Now everyone was chanting, '*Nama Mithras! Nama Mithras!*' At the same time they were shaking their Egyptian rattles. The chanting and the rattling and the strong smell of burning pine cones was making me dizzy. The chanting got faster and faster, louder and louder. As they reached a crescendo the other torch-bearer went behind the bull and pointed his torch down.

A great cheer erupted as the naked guy appeared from behind the cult statue. But he wasn't naked any more. Now he was wearing a new red tunic and a floppy orange hat. He looked dazed and happy and totally unharmed.

Dinu and I gawped at each other, wide-eyed.

'It must be magic!' said Dinu.

'Or a clever trick,' I replied.

That was when I noticed something.

The statue of Mithras had begun to glow with a pale shimmery light.

I came to my senses.

'Dinu!' I hissed. 'The portal is on! Go now – strip off and jump through. I'll be right behind you!'

He looked at me with big panicked eyes. 'I can't!' he said. 'I cannot get Lollia's ring off!'

51
Stella Sum

Whenever I think back to that moment, my skin crawls with horror. So many things could have gone wrong. So many things.

Dinu was looking at me with terrified Cleopatra eyes. 'I do want to go back!' he said. 'But I don't want my finger to explode.'

I looked at his left hand. The little finger was pink and swelling around the ring. I brought his hand closer as it was hard to see in the dim light of the smoky Mithraeum. I could see the ring was made of gold and was quite delicate. Could I bite through it?'

'Be brave!' I said. 'I'm going to try to bite it off.' I heard his gasp of pain as I closed my mouth around it and bit. This was no good; my teeth were pushing it in. I needed to cut through from inside. The knife! I pulled Mud Woman's knife out of my tunic belt and put the tip between the ring and his flesh. Blood oozed out and he whimpered and squeezed his eyes shut.

'Please God,' I prayed silently, 'help me do this and get us both back and I promise I will believe in You.' Then I gave the tip of the knife a violent twist. Dinu gasped. Blood spurted. Still the ring was not off.

But it was bent.

'Just once more,' I said, horribly aware that we were running out of time.

I pressed and gave the tip of the knife another twist. The ring snapped and fell to the stone floor with a ping.

Dinu's eyes were full of tears and his finger was bleeding, but at least he was still whole. 'Go! Go! Go!' I hissed.

As Dinu pulled off his tunic, I saw a second initiation was taking place in the central nave, right between us and the portal. A new naked guy was kneeling. This time the Father had a bow and arrow. As Dinu stepped out of his gladiator nappy and ran down the central nave, the Father pulled back the bowstring and let fly, aiming right at him.

By some miracle the arrow missed. I heard it strike the double oak doors of the Mithraeum with a *thunk*!

Meanwhile, Dinu had veered around the Father and the naked guy and jumped through the portal.

I almost cheered as he disappeared in a flash of green light.

Some of worshippers yelled in fear. Others cried out, *'Nama, Mithras!'*

A few of them fell forward in prayer. Or maybe they had just fainted.

The Father's dark eyes were as round as coins.

'Please, God!' I whispered. 'Please help me get through too, and please may we not have messed up the future!'

I dropped the bloody knife, untied my belt, peeled off my tunic and streaked down the central nave.

Don't ask me why, but just before I dived through the glowing disc of the time portal I yelled, '*Stella sum!*' I am a star!

52
President Trump

I forgot how awful it had been to go through the portal.

Once again every cell in my body felt like it was burning with cold fire.

Once again my eyes were glued shut.

But I was focused enough to yell, 'Turn it off! Turn off the portal now! The temple is full of men,' I added. 'One of them might try to come after us!'

I could barely hear my own voice above the high-pitched squealing noise that filled my head.

'It's OK,' said a female voice. 'It's off. Nobody else is coming through.'

I felt a woman's hands put a towel around me. Something cool and damp mopped my face and I caught the familiar smell of a wet wipe. Praise God! I was back in the twenty-first century!

But was it *my* twenty-first century? Or a twenty-first century where Germany had won World War Two, or maybe the Roman Empire had never fallen and everyone still spoke Latin.

Then, beyond the bat squeal in my ears, I heard more voices and a strange crackling noise. It sounded strangely like police walkie-talkies.

'Dinu! Are you here? Are you all right?'

'Yes, Alex. Are you?'

'I think so. Only my eyes are still stuck shut.'

'You probably want to keep eyes closed,' said Dinu. 'Is not pretty sight.'

'What's not a pretty sight?' I moaned. 'Didn't they have a towel big enough for you?'

I heard him laugh. 'Police are arresting Mr Daisy.'

'What?!'

'Yes. Also headteacher Miss Okonmah.'

I managed to open my right eye enough to see two policemen putting handcuffs on Solomon Daisy. Miss Okonmah was already in cuffs, with two WPCs standing nearby. A third was looking after me. The two tech guys, Geoff and Jeff, were not yet in cuffs, but they looked miserable.

'Are you sure the portal is off?' said a posh voice. A man in a suit stepped into my blurry field of vision. 'We don't want any extra-temporals coming through after them.'

'It's off, sir,' said Jeff with a J.

'Probably forever,' said Geoff with a G. 'It wasn't designed for two travellers.'

'Alex,' shouted Solomon Daisy as the police manhandled him out of the Mithraeum, 'did you find her?'

'Yes, sir!' I called back. 'Her name was Lollia Honorata. Her father was a retired auxiliary soldier turned spice merchant and her mother was a witch. She grew up in Lepcis Magna.'

'She was beautiful,' said Dinu.

'But Martin lied!' I added. 'He never left the Mithraeum. And we ended up interacting a lot. So you've got to tell us, did we change the future? Is Donald Trump still president?'

'You can rest easy,' said the man with the posh voice. 'Donald Trump is still president.'

'Thank God,' I breathed, as someone handed me a bottle of water.

The posh guy was looking down at me through his glasses. 'Tell me, did you really travel back in time?'

'Yes, sir,' I said between gulps of water.

'And you couldn't have changed that one small thing?'

53
Hazmat Men

Once when I was about eight and my parents were still alive, my dad was cleaning the cellar and he found a dead rat squashed under an old bed-frame. The rat had been dead so long that it was practically mummified. When my dad called the council to ask how he should dispose of a mummified rat, they said they would send someone right away.

Half an hour later the doorbell rang and when I opened the door I saw two spacemen in bright orange boiler suits with helmets on. I thought aliens had come to abduct us but Dad told me they were just men wearing hazmat suits. 'Hazmat' stands for 'hazardous materials' of course. Maybe they thought the mummified rat could be a carrier of bubonic plague or something like that.

Anyway, that memory came rushing back into my mind when they made me and Dinu put on bright orange hazmat suits. Then they helped us up the black marble time-stairs to a waiting ambulance. A quick glimpse of the dawn sky told me it was about eight o'clock in the morning. The area between the London Mithraeum and the Daisy Building was deserted and I remembered it was Saturday. Or maybe Sunday.

Once we were inside the ambulance, they put on the siren. I could tell we were going fast because we had to hang on around every corner.

After about ten minutes we went down a ramp and into an underground car park. Dinu and I were taken along a maze of concrete-floored corridors and finally into a windowless room where we had to take off the hazmat suits to be examined by doctors with their hazmat suits still on. The doctors checked us all over, using powerful torchlights on their foreheads and magnifying glass visors. They took swabs from inside our mouths. They tweezed the dirt from under our fingernails and toenails. They scraped stuff from behind our ears. They examined our heads like monkeys searching for ticks. They even took blood samples.

They also cleaned and bandaged Dinu's left pinkie finger where I had cut off the ring.

Then they ushered us into a kind of changing area with lockers and showers and toilet cubicles. They made us pee in cups and then left us alone with orders to take a very hot shower and scrub ourselves all over. Even in our ears.

Once we were dry, we found clothes laid out for us on a bench by a big mirror. We each got clean underwear, a brand-new pair of jeans, a black T-shirt and a grey hoodie. There were also some socks and black Adidas trainers. Everything fit us both perfectly.

'This is excellent,' said Dinu, pulling on his hoodie. 'I have never worn such nice new clothes before.'

We looked at our reflections in a big mirror.

I said. 'We look like mismatched twins. Like in that movie with the muscular bodybuilder and the little bald guy.'

'No,' said Dinu, running his fingers through still-damp hair, 'we look like Dionysus and Eros.'

'Yeah.' I grinned. 'You get to be a sexy grape god while I'm a dumb baby with wings.'

A man in a suit opened a door. He held the old-fashioned version of a touch tablet: a wooden clipboard.

'The doctors have given you the all-clear,' he said. 'Follow me.'

He led us along a corridor to a lift and sent us up about five floors. We emerged into another corridor – this one had carpet – and finally into a semicircular room with a very high ceiling. There was a round table in the centre and six chairs around it. Straight ahead of us were some tall, pale-green windows set on a curve and overlooking the river.

'Hey!' I said, going to the window. 'That's Vauxhall Bridge. I think we're inside MI6!'

'What is MI6?' asked Dinu.

'It's where the spies work, when they're not kissing beautiful double agents or getting cool new gadgets from Q.'

'What are gadgets from Q?'

'You know – from the James Bond films!'

'I know James Bond, but I do not know MI6.'

'It's famous,' I said. 'It's even in one of the recent Bond films. It's this modern building made of pale yellow stone and jade-green glass with a ziggurat vibe going on. People call it the Spy Building. Every Londoner knows it.'

Dinu went to the window and looked out. 'I have never heard of a Spy Building before.' He turned and looked around, then pointed at a CCTV camera in one corner of the room. 'But I know they are watching us.'

A moment later Mr Posh came in. He held the door open for three women to enter too. One had shoulder-length light brown hair. Another had short grey hair and a notebook. The third had a tray with tea things including biscuits and sandwiches. She put this on the table and went out, closing the door behind her.

'Please,' said Mr Posh with a smile, 'sit.'

I said, 'Is this the MI6 building? And is this a debriefing?'

'Precisely,' said Mr Posh, his smile getting broader. 'It won't take long. I promise to have you both home in time for tea. Speaking of which,' he went to the teapot, 'milk and sugar?'

We both nodded and he poured.

'Sophie?' he said.

'White please, no sugar,' said the woman with light brown hair.

'Jean?'

'White with two sugars,' said the grey-haired lady.

I'm pretty sure American secret agents get champagne and caviar for their debriefings. But the tea was hot and sweet and there were also those posh biscuits with chocolate on one side and also a plate of sandwiches cut in fancy triangles and with no crusts, so I didn't complain.

I looked around. 'Is it Saturday or Sunday?'

'Saturday lunchtime,' he said. 'You were gone twenty-four hours.'

As I bit into a cucumber-and-tuna sandwich on white bread, I realised it was the first food I had eaten in three or four days. I closed my eyes and savoured every bite.

When Dinu and I had taken the edge off our hunger, Mr Posh introduced the two women and then they questioned us for about two hours. The one with light brown hair was an archaeologist who told us to call her Dr Sophie. She asked us questions like 'What industry did you see in Southwark?' And 'How many people could the amphitheatre seat?'

The grey-haired woman's name was Jean. She said she was a nurse from social services. She asked if we had been in danger at any time or traumatised by anything we had seen.

Dinu and I glanced at each other and then began to laugh.

I counted on my fingers: 'I was chased by slaves, tripped up by a goat, nearly drowned in the Thames, attacked by a knife-wielding mud woman, kicked by kiln-slaves, pursued by angry female bath attendants and compared to Cupid.'

Dinu said, 'And I was dragged out of river, put in cell with smelly gladiators and made to fight.'

I added, 'That was only the beginning.'

Then we told them about our adventures, glossing over a lot.

About an hour into our debriefing, Dr Sophie leaned forward. 'You say Lollia's slave-girl was named Plecta?'

'Yes,' I said.

'I think that name appears on an inscription I've seen. I'm just going to ring a colleague at Mortimer Wheeler House,' she said. 'That's the Museum of London Archaeology Department.'

While she was out of the room Dinu and I slurped some more tea and wolfed down the last of the sandwiches, while Nurse Jean and Mr Posh scribbled notes. I was just brushing crumbs off my new jeans when Dr Sophie came back in.

She looked pale and the phone in her hand was trembling. But she was also smiling.

'I know what happened to Plecta,' she said.

54
Spirits of the Dead

'I was right,' said Dr Sophie. 'It's a very rare name, but it is attested in an epitaph from Londinium's northern cemetery.'

She showed us a photo on her phone. It was a tombstone and read:

> DIS MANIBVS
> LOLLIAE PLECTAE
> ANN XXXXII
> UXORI INCOMPARABILI
> MULIERI SANCTISSIMAE
> AELIUS CLAUDIUS EPAPRAS
> MARITUS OB MERITIS
> H S E S T T L

'What does it mean?' said Mr Posh. 'I only did Latin to GCSE level.'

'To the spirits of the dead,' said Dr Sophie, 'and of Lollia Plecta . . .'

'Lollia?' said Dinu, sitting up straight.

'Not your Lollia, I'm afraid,' said Dr Sophie with a sad smile. 'We still have her bones in the Museum of London and we know she died not long after you met her, perhaps within weeks.'

Dinu slumped in his seat.

'Do we know how she died?' I asked.

'No. And we may never know. But this inscription shows that Lollia, or perhaps Lollia's father, set Plecta free. According to the usual Roman practice, Plecta took Lollia's first name and kept her slave-name as her second name.'

Suddenly the sandwiches I'd eaten were going around in my stomach like clothes in a tumble-drier. 'Did she marry that fluffy-bearded lawyer who helped us set Dinu free?'

'Yes,' said Dr Sophie, 'I believe she did. Let me translate the whole thing. *To the spirits of the dead and of Lollia Plecta aged forty-two years, an incomparable wife and very clever woman. Her husband Aelius Claudius Epapras and her children did this because she deserved it.*' She took a breath. 'The last seven letters are an abbreviation for *Here she lies. May the earth lie lightly on you.*'

We were all quiet for a moment. Dinu was rooting in his pockets and Nurse Jean handed him a tissue. He used it to wipe his eyes and blow his nose.

'Forty-two is a ripe old age for those times,' said Dr Sophie. 'And she had children.' She looked at us. 'It may even be that one of us in this room is her descendent.'

'Not me,' said Dinu. 'I was born in Romania.' He blew his nose again and added, 'I wish we could have brought Lollia back to our time. I think she would have lived long time here.'

Nurse Jean patted his hand.

'It wouldn't have worked,' said Mr Posh. 'At best she wouldn't have been able to go through the portal. At worst she might have drastically changed all history at the moment of her crossing from the past to the present. That could have meant that none of us was born or that the Mithraeum was never replaced on its original site. It could even have caused the universe to collapse . . . That madman Solomon Daisy has been playing with something a billion times more dangerous than the most powerful bomb.'

At that moment a door opened and Martin limped in.

Mr Posh stood up and introduced him. Then he invited Martin to sit in the sixth chair.

For the next hour Mr Posh and Dr Sophie and Nurse Jean questioned him closely about his three visits to the past.

My theory had been correct.

Martin had never even peeped out of the Mithraeum. In fact, he hadn't really seen or heard that much about the mysterious goings on in the temple. Just about the masks and the clicking and some other strange noises.

'You made up all that stuff about a knife-seller named Caecilius with a shop near a pee laundry?' I asked him.

'Yes,' he admitted with a rueful shrug. 'I saw a documentary about ancient Rome once and never forgot that fact, that they used pee to clean clothes.'

'And I suppose you got the name Caecilius from the *Cambridge Latin Course*?' I said.

Martin shook his head. 'No, from *Doctor Who* – the episode where he goes back to Pompeii.'

'Did you know that Caecilius was a real Roman?' said Dr Sophie. 'He was a banker from Pompeii.'

The door opened and the tea lady came in with a fresh tray.

Martin said, 'When I came in you all looked like someone had died.'

'Only the whole universe,' I said, and added, 'Nearly.'

'You did the right thing by staying put,' said Mr Posh to Martin. 'You were far more sensible than these two.'

'Really?' said Martin, and for the first time he seemed to relax.

Mr Posh nodded grimly. 'The good news,' he said, 'is that, like in *Doctor Who*, your time travel doesn't seem to have disrupted the present.'

'Praise the Lord,' murmured the tea lady, who had been frozen by our discussion. She put down the new tray and took away the old one.

'Forget about destruction of universe!' cried Dinu. 'Here are salt-and-vinegar crisps!'

Sure enough, in addition to a fresh round of sandwiches there were three packets of crisps. Dinu and I each grabbed one.

The others seemed to have lost their appetites, but we grinned at each other and eagerly tucked in.

Mr Posh began to tell us some boring legal stuff about how the three of us had to check in regularly, and contact them urgently if we noticed any changes to our bodies.

'I'm almost thirteen,' I protested. 'I'm hoping for quite a few changes to my body.'

It was starting to get dark outside when the lights came on in the round room. They told us we were almost done.

We only had to sign about a dozen forms, including one called the Official Secrets Act, which is why I haven't given you the real names of Mr Posh or Dr Sophie or Nurse Jean from social services.

'Solomon Daisy recruited your headteacher with a cool three mil in an offshore account,' said Mr Posh, 'I believe he promised you a great deal of money too. But as you know, he's been arrested and it will be a long time before he or his assets are free again.'

'So no five million?' I said.

'I'm afraid not,' said Mr Posh, and reached into his jacket.

He pulled out two envelopes and tossed them onto the table. 'I've put some money from petty cash in those envelopes, just to cover your expenses.'

'Two hundred pounds!' said Dinu, counting his out. His face shone.

'Of course you can keep your new clothes too,' said Mr Posh. 'Also –' he slid two smartphones across the polished surface of the table – 'always keep those with you in case we need to get in touch. If you remember anything important or suffer any sickness, nightmares or panic attacks, don't hesitate to call me.' He stood up, rested both hands on the table and leaned towards me and Dinu. 'I particularly want you to get in touch at once if you notice anything different about the world now compared to what it was before your trip. You are the only two who will know if actions in the past affected our current world. My number is already in your contacts list under Uncle Harry.'

'I'm Aunt Jean,' said the social worker.

'And I'm Dr Sophie,' said Dr Sophie.

'Remember,' said Mr Posh, 'you've signed the Official Secrets Act. You can't tell anybody what you saw in the past, not even your parents or guardians.'

'But we can talk to each other, right?' said Dinu.

'Of course,' said Mr Posh. 'Now, who would like that last packet of crisps?'

Dinu and I both lunged for it, but Dinu was faster.

He pulled it open and hesitated.

Then he grinned and offered the pack to me. 'No more bully,' he said. 'We share?'

55
Hashtag Snowpocalypse

It was snowing the next day. The whole country freaked out over a few centimetres of cold white stuff. People were calling it #Snowpocalypse and posting film clips of their dogs going bonkers, or Photoshopping ginormous Walkers from *Star Wars* stalking the streets of sleepy English villages.

They closed our school that Monday. They declared it a #SnowDay. Dinu came round and the two of us tried to kick a football up on the common. But it was too slippery, so we built a snow zombie outside my block of flats and then attacked it with snowballs.

When Dinu first arrived at my house he was wearing a thin windcheater, so I lent him my dad's old puffer jacket. It fit him perfectly, and when we came in laughing and stamping the snow off our feet, Gran said he could keep it.

He was so pleased that he gave her a hug, so she invited

him to stay for dinner. Dinu phoned home to ask, and his mum said he could as long as he was home by nine.

The flat was warm and cosy. Gran's multicoloured hippy lamps made the old Turkish carpet look new. Her ferns seemed to glow from inside, like emeralds or something. She even turned on the little gas fire with the fake coals that looked like rubies.

While Gran made good smells in the kitchen, Dinu and I played the latest zombie game on my old PlayStation. For a while it was fun, but soon we turned it off and talked about Lollia and Plecta.

'I really liked her,' said Dinu. 'I wish we had brought her back.'

'Me, too,' I said. 'Both of them. We could have taken them to a dentist and got their teeth cleaned.'

'Let them try pizza and chocolate,' said Dinu.

'And taken them to school as our girlfriends,' I added. 'Their balance-beam double act would be a sensation on YouTube.'

Gran came in carrying a casserole dish. She was using the Darth Vader oven mitts I had got for her last birthday.

We sat down and tucked in. Dinu loved the giant beans in tomato sauce. He had three helpings and told us about a pet goat he used to have in Romania. It was called Vlad and it ate everything in sight.

'You should have called him Vlad the Inhaler,' I said.

Dinu didn't get it, but Gran laughed so hard she almost fell off her chair.

After dinner she challenged Dinu to a game of backgammon.

While they were playing I did the dishes and then thought I might as well do Saturday's chores as I had been otherwise occupied that day. So I put on my rubber gloves, grabbed the bathroom cleaner and sponge scourer and went at the bathtub.

I polished the old chrome taps until they came up as shiny as silver. The turquoise tub gleamed, and when I turned on the showerhead to rinse off the soap I had a revelation. As a spray of clean hot water came out I realised that the richest Roman could never dream of the luxury of this bathroom in our little two-bedroom flat.

Then I opened the medicine cabinet and looked at the treasures within. Paracetamol for a headache or bad sprain. Savlon to stop a cut from getting infected. Toothpaste with fluoride to strengthen my teeth and keep them pearly white. Gran's disposable contact lenses so she could see without wearing glasses. The prescription medicine that had added maybe two decades to her life. And a spare roll of puppy-soft Andrex for wiping your bottom.

A rich widow or wealthy merchant from Roman Londinium would probably give everything they owned to possess the contents of this cabinet.

'Hey, Wimpy!' came Dinu's voice from the other room. 'I just beat your gran at backgammon. Now I challenge you.'

'You're on!' I yelled back. 'I'm going to crush you.'

'I'm making hot chocolate,' called Gran from the kitchen. 'With whipped cream on top.'

I closed the mirrored door of the cabinet and told myself, 'You're not wimpy. You are Eros, the god of love.'

Then I gave the bathroom a final fond glance. Later that night I would take a mango bubble bath and clean every inch of my body. Then I would wash my hair with coconut-scented shampoo and pineapple-enhanced conditioner before rinsing it with lovely warm water. Finally I would slip in between crisp sheets with a goose-down duvet to keep me toasty warm.

But for now there was hot chocolate, a board game and a good friend waiting.

The end

. . . or is it?

AUTHOR'S NOTE

In case you are in any doubt, this story is made up. It never happened. However, some of it is based on real facts, especially the parts about the girl with the ivory knife. Archaeologists really did find her bones on Lant Street in Southwark, a few minutes' walk south of the Tate Modern. DNA analysis really did tell us her eye colour and stable isotope analysis indicated the place where she might have grown up. The ivory knife, wooden box and little glass bottles were all found buried with her. We know she had bandy legs that were getting better. We don't know her name, her story or how she died. I made all those things up.

One fact I bent a little is the location of London's recently re-opened Mithraeum. Although it is very close to the original position, it is off by a few metres.

You could take the same facts about the Mithraeum and the Lant Street Teenager and make up a completely different story.

One of the differences between an archaeologist and an author is that an archaeologist has to stick to the facts, but an author can use their imagination to create a story. The report on the bones or the DNA of the girl with the ivory knife is fairly dry, and there are lots of gaps showing what we don't know. But I am very grateful to the scientists and lab technicians who gave us the reports, and especially to bioarchaeologist Dr Rebecca Redfern.

I would love to go back 1800 years to Roman London and meet the girl with the ivory knife and find out her real story. But time travel will probably never happen, so in the meantime our imaginations are the best portals we have to the past.

Caroline Lawrence

Caroline Lawrence's Roman Mysteries books were first published in 2001 and have since sold over a million copies in the UK alone, and been translated into fourteen languages. The series was televised by the BBC in 2007 and 2008 with ten half-hour episodes per season. Filmed in Tunisia, Bulgaria and Malta, it was the most expensive BBC children's TV series to date.

Caroline says: 'I want to know everything about the past, especially the exciting things. Also the sounds, smells, sights and tastes. I write historical novels because nobody has invented a Time Machine. And I write for kids because eleven is my inner age.'

Visit Caroline's website: www.carolinelawrence.com

Look for the next adventure in

THE TIME TRAVEL DIARIES

series

Coming in January 2020

And don't miss . . .

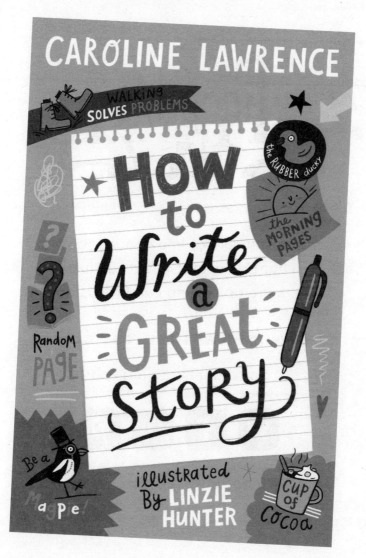

Coming in August 2019

PRESS

Thank you for choosing a Piccadilly Press book.

If you would like to know more about our authors, our books or if you'd just like to know what we're up to, you can find us online.

www.piccadillypress.co.uk

You can also find us on:

We hope to see you soon!